TRUTH HUNTER

BOOK FIVE

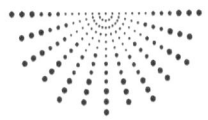

KATRINA COPE

COSY BURROW BOOKS

AFTERLIFE BOOKS

Truth Hunter

eBook first published in USA in April 2020 by Katrina Cope

eBook first published in Great Britain in April 2020 by Katrina Cope

www.katrinacopebooks.com

Published by Katrina Cope

All rights reserved

ASIN: B085G3LRRZ

❀ Created with Vellum

To all the lovely people going through hell on Earth.
May you find the magic in your life.

PROLOGUE

I t burns—a deep seething pain, shooting through the core of my body and springing to my skin. Oh, sweet angel, it burns. Anger, despair, guilt, regret, depression, and longing for my lost loved ones. It's like a furnace cranked so hot it explodes deep in my stomach, causing my fury and misery to burst forth like lava from a volcano. I can't believe it happened to me again. First my birth parents, then my guardian parents, and now my beloved husband, Jehan—all of them slaughtered, taken from me, their souls disappearing into oblivion, leaving me behind with the torment. To add to my distress, my guardian—I heard of his misfortune, and it tears me apart, adding to the furnace of anguish brewing within my soul. Zacharias, literally my guardian angel for a large part of my young life, has lost his wings—severed by a demon.

It was difficult for Archangel Michael to get the message through to me in my current condition. It was apparent he didn't want to tell me because of my emotional and physical state. Except he was desperate for my help. *Huh! I can't even help myself.*

Zacharias is safe, but he dredges through an emotional marsh. The knowledge throws me deeper into this shape I shifted into.

At the moment, I'm not sure I want to remove my anger and the urge for revenge, and until I do, I cannot change back into my human form. I'm stuck in this green body mass with all its power, flying the skies as a lost soul.

Diving from the sky, I land on the highest mountain, and I roar to my heart's content, shooting large plumes of fire. Still, it doesn't calm my soul. Somehow, I have to find inner peace. Even though I know that Zacharias needs me right now, I can't do it, which means I can't go to the Tatev Monastery. Not only would I scare the monks and any visiting people, I wouldn't be able to fit down the halls. I haven't visited the monastery before, but I'm sure they can't accommodate a dragon walking down the hallways. I wouldn't be a comfort to Zacharias in this form anyway. No. Right now, I'm nobody's comforter, only my own tormentor. A person who cannot comfort themselves would be no use cheering anybody else.

I try to focus on something calming, anything that will relax me. My mind focuses and lands on my favorite chicken, Mademoiselle, and I think of how I gathered her into my arms many times when I was upset. I can't do that now. In this form, I would only scare her. The image of her in my arms as I stroke her brown feathers enters my head. It calms me until I remember that Mademoiselle has long passed and was a part of my farm, the farm where I grew up with Zacharias overseeing me, the farm where I brought Jehan when Zacharias moved out and we started to live as a married couple. Our peaceful lives fell apart too quickly, at the same time, tearing out my soul, removing all chances of peace.

Anger sears within my soul and into the pit of my stomach, spurting through my body. The pulse is consistent, angry energy pounding into every single limb, right down to the tips of my wings and the points of my talons.

I push off the mountaintop, extending my long, green wings, and flap. I love flying—although it currently voids all comfort. For all I know, I'm trapped in this form, unable to help Zacharias unless I manage to stumble across the gatekeeper. Involuntarily, the corner of my mouth lifts in a smirk, showing off my dragon teeth. I would love to give him a little of his own treatment. I'm unlikely to see him soon. He has no interest in me.

The evil little gatekeeper has destroyed all the people that I care for, affecting everybody that I love. I have no one else he can take. In my mind, I've almost beckoned him to take me and punish me, to do his worst. I wish he would give back Zacharias's wings and let me take his place. I'm sure his role in this life is more important than mine. Yet, here I am. Weeks have passed, and I'm still stuck in this massive, giant, green dragon form, trapped in my torment, destined to stay like this until I gain control of my emotions.

I wish there were a switch to transform out of this dragon form. It's new to me, and I haven't mastered the transformation yet.

I've flown the skies of France, tormenting the people as I pass over the villages. In some weird way, it satisfies me when I see them panic. I guess I want as much destruction passed on to them as I've had in my life. Surely, not one of them has had as much trauma in their life as what I've dealt with in my short twenty-one years. I cannot comprehend anyone having the bad luck I've had.

After several more weeks, the anger slowly dies down. It's dawning on me that I'm not achieving anything by remaining a dragon. The angry dragon made me feel better for a while, but it's not constructive. It doesn't take away my pain except for the slight dullness that the overexertion brought.

CHAPTER ONE

Forgiveness calms the soul—or so they say. I wouldn't know. I don't think I could ever forgive, but somehow, I have to. I must pull myself together for Zacharias's sake. He needs me, and if I'm honest, I also need him. I have to remind myself that the days of my childhood are over. I must learn to deal with my grief and turn it around to help others.

Somehow, Michael managed to break through my torment to give me the message that Zacharias is in a bad state and desperately needs my help.

I wish I could take Zacharias's pain from him. He is immortal and must live the rest of his life without his wings unless they find them and he can be healed—a feat that seems impossible. I have spent weeks in my dragon form, watching the sun rise and set, displaying its full magnificence.

That's enough. I must learn to control myself. Why is it taking so long? I thought I was stronger than this. I have suffered such grief before. The only difference is I haven't possessed the ability to let the dragon form take hold of me every time I lost control of my emotions.

I land on a green mountaintop and take in the scenery—slowly breathing in and out, trying to calm my soul. It takes quite some time before calmness creeps under my skin and slowly dissolves the anger. After one final long, deep breath in and out, my body disintegrates into particles and whirls into a circle before forming into my human body.

It's cold on the mountaintop, especially in my thin shape-shifting clothes. I rub my arms, traveling as quickly as I can on the long trek down the mountainside, returning to the place I used to call home.

With each step, my apprehension grows. I'm not sure it's such a good idea to return to my farm, but I don't know where else to go. Maybe a long walk down the mountainside will calm me further. Perhaps, when I arrive at the farm, I will quickly grab my essential things and go somewhere else. I just hope the archangels had the decency to bury my beautiful Jehan instead of leaving him on the table where he was tortured by the gate-keeper. If Jehan is still there, I will fall apart. Surely the angels would remember to look after my late husband's body, even though they are distracted by Zacharias.

I reach a rugged place and move to all fours, climbing down the rocky surface, using my hands as well as my feet. I'm impressed I've managed to stay out of my dragon form for as long as I have. I must be regaining control of my temperament and managing how I feel. Encouragement churns inside of me. I must do this. I have to do this for myself because nobody else can. There's nobody else to pull me out of this oblivion, not with Zacharias and Jehan gone. Jehan was the only human I could turn to. He was my resort when I needed help, and now he's gone.

I reach the bottom of the hill and enter the forest. I know somewhere in the middle is my farm and cabin. I've been living off pickings on the mountainside, eating whatever flesh creature came my way. It'll be a welcome change to live off my garden and my meat supply—although I haven't had to kill my animals before. When I was younger, Zacharias prepared my meals until I met Jehan.

The thought of them broken and gone brings hot tears to my eyes. Thankfully, I don't revert back into my dragon form. I wipe away the wet streaks that run freely down my face.

Almost scared to open the door, I approach the cottage with caution. The porch creaks as I step on the planks, each one playing a different tune. I was hoping to approach the door without a sound, as ridiculous as it seems. I long to sneak up on my place and surprise the torment lying inside.

Clasping the handle of the door, I pause and take long, deep breaths. My heart races as I enter, dreading what could confront me. I steel myself, bracing against every emotion and locking them away. It must be done.

I look straight at the table, letting out a large breath from the depths of my lungs. It's bare.

"Thank you," I mutter, thinking of the archangels. They cleared away my beautiful Jehan. Hopefully, they buried him somewhere respectable that I can visit. From my years with Zacharias and the other archangels' occasional visits, I am sure they have covered these needs.

Pulling my eyes away from the empty table, I progress inside. It took every bit of courage to get this far. I'm not going to give up now. It's not the first time I've been through the hardship. I can get through it again.

It torments me as I remember Zacharias's words from when I was younger, before I started dating Jehan. He said that it's better to experience love and loss over our lives. It's better to live life to the fullest by knowing them.

They were powerful words. So much so, that they convinced me to get to know Jehan and hold a deep relationship with him. I don't regret a single day I spent with him. My only remorse is that he was taken from me so soon. I was ready to have his children and live my life with him, watch him grow older along with our children. Instead, the gatekeeper brought his demons to our farm before we had a chance to live that life. Not only that, he took Zacharias and punished him beyond anything an archangel should ever have to endure. I can only imagine the torment would make him wish he had died instead. I need to visit him.

No sooner did I step through my doorway than

Archangel Michael visited. His golden breastplate and his Roman uniform gleam as he stands in the center of the doorway I was too scared to shut—afraid of being tormented with Jehan's remains.

After I went so long without seeing any of the protection archangels, his robust image, framed by the light from outside, reminds me of my warrior and protector, my wonderful Zacharias. My knees wobble, and I want to break down and cry. Instead, I bite my lip and look directly at Archangel Michael.

"Where is Jehan?" Steeling my emotions makes my eyes narrow at the archangel.

"We buried him in the field." The usually stern archangel's blue eyes are wrought with compassion and understanding. He's the perfect warrior—fierce, yet when necessary, he can show his gentle side. "He's not far from the cottage." He places a hand on my upper arm, the gesture warm and comforting. "Don't worry. We looked after him. He means as much to us as you do." He rubs my shoulder. "And you mean a great deal. Not only have you been like Zacharias's daughter, you also helped defend us against the demons and stopped them from overtaking the humans." His eyes are earnest. "Ava, we need you back. Zacharias needs you."

My shoulders slump forward, and I close my eyes, the exhaustion of the last few weeks threatening to take over. "I know. I know he needs me." I gaze at Archangel Michael. "And I need him. It's taken a lot of effort to get this far."

"I know. Is there anything we can do to help?" Worry clads his sapphire-blue eyes.

"No. Only I can work through this." I face the inside of the cottage. "Thank you for burying Jehan. It means a lot to me."

"Oh, Ava. Of course, we would bury him. I would hate for you to return to that. He deserved so much more, as do you. I'm sorry that being involved with us has gotten you into this mess."

I suck in a deep, staggered breath, the air struggling to get past my emotions. "If it weren't for you, I wouldn't have met Jehan in the first place. It's because of Zacharias and his persistence that I met Jehan, and you sent Zacharias here to protect me my whole life. I don't blame you for what happened." I breathe slowly and deeply then look into the archangel's eyes. "I'm ready to see Zacharias now. Take me to him. Please."

Archangel Michael nods once then grabs hold of my hand. My body disintegrates as we teleport then reforms a few seconds later outside a building built with dull gray stones.

"Where are we?" The awed whisper escapes my lips as I gaze past the edge of the mountain, blown away by the view of the valley. The hills roll in green waves. The valleys are deep and beautiful—a contrast to the dull gray stone building behind me. I face the building. A large cross sits at the peak of the spire. The front door is an open stone canopy securing the roof with several tall pillars.

I don't hear Archangel Michael answer, and I ask,

"What is this place? The valley is magnificent, and the building has its own charm, but the gray stones hold an air of depression." My fingers run over the gray stone, feeling its roughness. The natural materials would most likely have been the only building materials available when they built it.

"This is the Tatev Monastery. It is one of the many monasteries held within Armenia."

I stare at him, wondering what the significance of this is.

"We keep Zacharias here and gave him an essential role to assist the angels. He protects something very important to us, and to do this, he must spend much time deep within the confines of the monastery, an area built by angels deep within the Tatev mountain in a spot that only approved monks and angels can go."

He rocks up on his toes, and the flaps of his Roman warrior's uniform sway with the movement. "I must visit him now. These visits have been painful for him and for me. As important as his new duty is, he doesn't see it as such. I'm afraid that the loss of his wings has sent him into deep depression and anger."

A shiver runs down my spine as I connect with the devastation I imagine Zacharias feels. "I can understand that." I rub my upper arm, trying to settle my tingling skin.

"And I too. I understand the pain he is going through, but he needs to move past it. No matter what I do, I can't pull him out of his anger and lust for revenge. Only he can do that, and I don't think he is going to do it anytime soon." He expels a massive sigh, and the edges of his mouth turn down farther. "I will go down and see if I can bring him up to the surface. I can't guarantee it. Even if he doesn't come up to see you, thank you for coming."

He turns around and disappears into the monastery, leaving me standing in the middle of the grass field. The abandonment hurts, but I think of Zacharias and how much of a father he is to me, and I wait. As much as I wish he would grant me access to this secret area, I understand that Michael is treading on tenterhooks.

I have seen Zacharias's fighting ability. He possesses a deep spirit, and the thought of him being spiteful and vengeful with those skills is scary. I can imagine how everyone who approaches him could be in danger. Even to his best brother, the one and only archangel he served without question. As an adopted daughter, I wouldn't be any safer, so I wait on the grass plain. He will be difficult, maybe even more obstinate than I am.

To fill the void in time, I take in the view, using its magnificence to calm myself. I can see how this place could be therapeutic if Zacharias came to the surface for a short period each day. It's soothing, like the views from the hilltops of France.

Breathing in deeply, I try to push aside my impatience and anxiety as I wait for the archangels to arrive.

CHAPTER TWO

Remaining here, taking in the beautiful view, didn't make time go by any faster. I wouldn't be surprised if I'd only been waiting a few seconds in my anticipation of Zacharias's arrival. My nerves over seeing what state he's in and how he will interact with me is making the time drag out. I wish Archangel Michael would hurry up.

I stare into the distance and look past the plain. On the other side of the rock wall, the land seems to drop away, tumbling or cascading down into the deep valley below. It's impressive how high the monastery is on this mountain.

The valley is a deep beautiful green and seems to flow forever. If I weren't so nervous waiting for Michael's return, I wouldn't fight the temptation to turn into my eagle form and take to the sky. The waiting is probably a good thing. I'm still fickle in my emotions, and it's best I remain in my human form. Changing in and out of my shape-shifting forms—especially the flying ones—when I'm on the brink of reverting to my dragon form indefinitely would not be wise. I cannot take that chance until my emotions calm down.

I only hope I can keep it together when I see Zacharias and observe the state that I've heard he's in. Just thinking about it sets my heart burning. The warmth of the dragon form travels rapidly beneath my skin, and I feel the scales prickling just underneath the surface. Dragon vision flashes in front of my eyes. I close them and take deep, slow breaths, forcing the vision to subside and not rear its head. I love my dragon form, but right now, it's not the best form for me.

Grass crackles behind me. I turn and spot Archangel Michael exiting the Tatev Monastery. His golden breast-plate gleams in the sun, but his eyes don't reflect the sun's brightness. Instead, they study the ground, and I know the outcome of his visit to my guardian just by looking at his body language.

"He won't come?" I ask.

Archangel Michael shakes his head and slowly lifts his eyes to look at me. The sorrow hits me like a slap on the face.

"No. He won't." He rubs my upper arm comfortingly, as though he's read my emotions. "But I'm certain it's not you. He's so consumed by anger that he won't hear reason from anyone."

I peer past him at the entrance of the monastery, studying the dark interior as though Zacharias will eventually follow anyway. I don't see him. The entrance remains black and empty, and my heart lowers to my stomach. I was desperately looking forward to seeing him again. I hoped to show my support for him and to give back to him after everything he has done for me over my lifetime. I hoped it would lift his spirits, but I can't do that if he doesn't come. It's almost like he's using his angelically blessed room to hide. I wish he would make an effort to come halfway. I long to embrace and comfort him, like he did when I lost my parents. I could use his comfort again, too, after the loss of Jehan, but I'm willing to put that on a back burner to help Zacharias. He has lost so much also. Remembering his steadfast and robust personality, I hang on to the hope that eventually he'll come back and find the fighter in himself.

I look at Archangel Michael again. "Are you sure he won't come out?"

The archangel studies his boots, and it takes a moment for him to shake his head. When he finally looks up, I'm taken aback by how much sadness and regret fill his sapphire eyes.

I place a hand on Michael's upper back, under his majestic white wings, the back of my hand brushing against the soft feathers. "He will come out of it eventually. He's a fighter. I've never seen him give up, even when he's completely lost."

Michael nods, yet the sadness remains fixed in his expression. "This time it's bad. He's so angry, a trait you never see in angels." His shoulders slump, and I rub his upper back between the arches of his majestic white wings, trying to offer some comfort. "I don't blame him, but it's an unusual trait." He glances over the valley for a few moments before he sighs. "Come, Ava. We must go. There's no point waiting here. We have much to get done, and you have more recovering to do." He grabs my arm, and we teleport back to the farm.

Over the next few weeks, we make these trips on several more occasions. Zacharias refuses me every single visit. The last time, Archangel Michael comes out of the Tatev Monastery shaking his head, his sapphire-blue eyes swimming with a sadness that travels so deep, I didn't think it possible. "He keeps claiming that you're not here, Ava. He refuses to leave the room to see for himself because he is accusing me of trying to trick him. For some reason, he thinks we want him gone. This is far from true. I wish I could take away his pain."

My heart sinks when the protector angel tells me this. I've lost count of how many times we have visited him and he's refused to see me. "Perhaps it's time I give it a break. Perhaps my visits are aggravating him, reminding him of my childhood and what his life should be like and how happy his life once was."

Michael returns me to the farm once again. I plod around, doing my daily tasks and caring for the animals, but the joy isn't there. My small farm can't cheer me up anymore. My favorite chicken, Mademoiselle, has passed away after many years. I have many animals left, but I just can't find peace. At every farm I lived on, my loved ones were ripped away from me—

brutally murdered one way or another. I don't sleep in the cottage anymore. I moved to the barn.

The cottage has become a constant reminder of Jehan and Zacharias. Good memories that I no longer partake in. Memories that only lead me to depression. I close myself away in the barn for several hours, giving up on happiness, and don't even take pleasure in feeding the animals. Each day I set up another spell to automatically feed them so they are cared for and looked after.

My life continues like this, day after day, until one day it hits me that I'm acting precisely like Zacharias. This isn't what life is about.

My heart grows restless. I can't stay here. There are too many memories, and I don't want to live the rest of my life alone on this little farm. I have too many questions I want answered.

I fetch some eggs from the chicken pen, and a chicken runs up to me. I squat down and stroke its back. Yes, it's time to find out some answers. As much as I love my animals and my little farm, I want to know where my life began. I need to understand why it's filled with so much trouble and torment. At one stage, Mama and Papa had mentioned where I'd come from. Now that I have my powers and shape-shifting ability, I'm stronger. I think it's a good time to return to my birthplace and investigate what happened to them there.

A nervous hope that there are others like me swirls within my stomach. Yet I know that if they aren't like me, then they could be humans who want to burn me at the stake. If this is how my life turns out, then so be it. I no longer have anything to live for except to find answers to these questions. I deserve to know how my life began and if there are others like me and what they can do with their witch and shape-shifting abilities. One day we may all be allies or enemies. It's best to find out now.

CHAPTER THREE

I consider calling into my parents-in-law's place to tell them my plans then decide against it. It's best I leave without telling them, or I'll have to put up with them worrying about my mental health and the well-being of the farm. They don't know I'm a shape-shifting witch. Only Jehan knew. It would be hard to explain to them that I'll feed the animals magically while I'm away. Instead, I spend the day walking on the farm and ensuring that each animal has a spell to feed, water, and protect it every single day. I don't want the animals to suffer. Besides, I might need this farm one day, or perhaps somebody in need will stumble across it and use all of its goods.

When done, I cast a spell over my spell books to make them diminish to the size of a small rock that will fit neatly inside the palm of my hand. I collect the bag that Jehan made and throw my few things into it, including my two spell books. Slinging it over my shoulder, I look for a way to travel. I want to take my few meager possessions with me, so I can't travel in my animal form. I toss ideas around in my head, wondering what to do. I've never made myself a broomstick, nor have I met any witches to see what their broomsticks look like.

I observe the broomstick I enchanted to sweep the floor of my cottage. As much as it is useful and attractive for a broom, it's too big. I don't want to lug it around everywhere. I would look suspicious walking into a village from a forest carrying a broomstick. In an age where they burn witches at the stake, I must find something different to use. Whatever I take must be small and able to fit in my bag or somewhere on me that will go unnoticed. After searching the cupboards and looking through the forest, I come up empty. I don't know what to use. Standing in the middle of the porch, I gaze around the yard, and my hand instinctively goes to my neck and wraps around a small charm hanging there. As my fingers linger over the charm, so many emotions surge through me. I don't have to look down to know how the beautiful golden leaves hang neatly from a thin golden chain.

Tears well in my eyes, threatening to break free. Zacharias made this chain and charm for me from his golden breastplate. He made it to be an object that I could use to call on Zacharias whenever I was in trouble. So far, I haven't used it. I forgot it existed when I needed it the most because it was new at the time, and I was in so much torment. Right now, with the way

Zacharias is, he would be unable to come even if he wanted to. That doesn't make the charm any less valuable. It still holds an essential place in my heart.

As I stand with my hand wrapped around it, a warm trickle runs down the side of my nose, and salty water tickles my lips. I wipe it away with my spare hand, and a thought enters my head. I have the magic to adapt my necklace, and I have a brilliant idea. I unclasp the hook from behind my neck and let the charm drop into my hands. Warm emotions flood through me as I cradle it with loving care.

I close my eyes and will the gold chain to combine and condense and form into a straight pin attached to the golden leaves. After the straight pin forms, I will it to bend forward and hook underneath the leaves, turning it into a beautiful golden-leaf bobby pin. When certain it's complete, I open my eyes and slide it into my hair. It fits perfectly, securing the loose strands of my golden-blond hair that have fallen out of my braid.

Removing the pin from my hair, I look at it again, flipping it over in my hand a few times. The sturdiness impresses me, instilling a satisfaction that it will be strong enough to do the job.

With my hand open, I whisper words of magic and blow upon its golden surface, casting a spell over the pin. After a few moments, I repeat the enchantment, watching as the hooked piece of pin flips out as though it's a latch. With my spare hand, I stretch it out, lining it up in the opposite direction to the leaves. The pin grows, extending past my flat palm and beyond. The golden leaves reach in the opposite direction and fade to brown, changing from leaves to long spindly pieces.

Even though I was the one who cast the spell, my eyes widen in wonder as the pin grows into a broomstick. Despite the sadness I carry, I can't help but chuckle with joy. I'm amazed at what magic can do when guided in the right direction.

There's one last thing. I clasp the broom in both my hands, holding it out in front of me, and whisper another enchantment. The broomstick illuminates briefly and twinkles around the edge for a split second.

Anxiety swirls in my stomach, and I close my eyes. I hope it works. Prying my eyes open, I look at the broomstick and tilt my head to the side, raising one eyebrow. Nothing seems to be different about the broomstick.

"There's only one way to find out," I mutter to myself, rising to my feet and walking into the middle of the yard. I hook the broom between my legs then visualize it flying. It lifts. With a shaky start, it moves forward. Lifting my feet off the ground, I hook my legs over the brushy part of the broomstick and travel a few feet. I barely manage to pull up at the last second, just before I hit the pigpen. The collision would've hurt. My aim changes straight into the air, and quickly I adjust, attempting to level out so I head forward, not up.

It takes a while to get ahold of this form of flying. It's not as though I'm using wings that are part of my body. I'm learning to control an object I must rely on to fly.

Within moments, I loop around and find myself heading straight at the cottage. At the last second, I tilt but not before I nick the outside corner. It sets me off balance, and I crash to the ground, landing with a thud. Groaning in pain, I slowly push myself to a sitting position. Thankfully the cottage wasn't high.

Despite the faint pain, I can't help but laugh as I watch the broom continue its course around the cottage. Flying the broom is actually fun—challenging and a skill that needs perfecting, but fun.

The practice lasts several more hours before I master the skill enough to start on the road. Hoisting my bag and threading it over my shoulders, I'm about to leave the farm when I realize that I don't know where to go. I haven't traveled anywhere besides the few random spots that the angels teleported me to in order help them fight or to the town where Jehan lived. I must visit a village to see if I can find out where Vezelay, my birth town, is and which direction I need to travel.

CHAPTER FOUR

My travels take me from one village to the next, and I land my broomstick in the seclusion of the bushes. Each time, I fold my broomstick away and slide it into my hair as a pin before entering the village with my bag on my back. In each village, I purchase the things I need and ask questions as to where I need to go. I have no idea which direction Vezelay lies, and as I travel through the villages, that seems to be a common theme as I repeat my questions over and over. Sometimes the answer is vague, and sometimes I'm sent to the next village. Accurate information is hard to come by, and often my frustration rises, making it hard to be pleasant.

The sun rises and sets several times, and I still haven't found my old village. North is the direction that most people give, and I follow their instructions. Although frustrated, I'm not angry at the humans. I know they don't have any mode of communication or transport other than walking, horse, or donkey— prolonged methods of travel.

A caravan of merchants sells their goods in the next town, and my hopes rise. I've heard merchants travel far and wide and will be the best people to ask when seeking information about different locations. A man not much taller than my waist attempts to strap a horse's chest to the carts. They look to be going on another trip.

"Excuse me," I call, moving closer to the short man.

He glances at me then eyes me slowly from head to toe. His eyes are a muddy brown, embedded in a weathered and worn face. A dagger swings in its sheath hanging from his belt. Eventually, his eyes pause on my face. "Yes?"

"I was looking for Vezelay. Do you know which direction I must go?"

His mouth tilts up into a half smile, making my skin crawl. Even though it makes me feel uncomfortable, I leave it alone.

"Traveling, are we?" He peers around my body, as if looking for something behind me. "Alone." His smirk broadens. "It's a shame that you're not heading in the same direction as us. You could come along with our convoy and keep me company."

A shiver runs down my spine all the way to my coccyx.

"Such a shame," I say sarcastically. "Can you point me in the right direction?"

Even though I cringe, I see the irony of it. If this man

knew what I could do, he wouldn't talk to me like that. His creepiness almost makes me want him to make an inappropriate move so I can show him. I could easily kill him or disfigure him more than he already is.

I shove the thought aside and focus on my goal. "Do you know where it is?"

He nods and points again in an odd direction. "It is about ten villages that way. You're not far now. Are you sure you wouldn't like to change your mind and join me? A girl like you needs looking after."

I'm short in comparison to most women my age, a feature that is very misleading when it comes to my strengths and gifts. I cock an eyebrow. "I would be too much animal for you to bear."

He smirks. "It's just the way I like them."

I shake my head. "I'm going now. Thank you for the directions." I leave him standing with his horses.

I can't get out of there quick enough. The little man was no threat to me, but he was disgusting and gave me the creeps. Knowing I need more supplies, I stop at a stall and buy a large bowl of stew, some fresh bread, and fruit. I'm thankful that I don't have to eat any dried food for a couple of days. It could be days of traveling, but if the little man was telling the truth, at least the end is near.

A mind reading gift like the angels have would come in handy, but that's one gift I don't possess. Maybe I can work on that later. Without Zacharias and Jehan by my side, I need to be more assertive. I can't see inside of these people. Maybe there is a spell I can create to do so, but I would have to create another to wipe their memory after I've done it. I can't have people knowing that I read their minds. As I think it over, I frown then shrug—one spell at a time.

The forest not far from the village is a tangled mess of long branches and trunks. Animal calls sound from all directions, yet I'm not afraid, not even of the dangerous animals. I know I can change into one of them—or something more vicious—or fly to a tree. Whatever suits me at the time to get away from them.

A small clearing opens before me, and my stomach growls. Sitting on a rock nearby, I pull the bag off my shoulders. Absentmindedly, I slide the golden pin farther into my hair, thinking that I will have to unfold it to increase my pace. First, though, I need to eat. While I sit on a rock and gnaw at some fruit, something shimmers in the corner of my eye. Blue particles roll around in a circle, forming into a column until, eventually, they develop into an angel. Worry lines the usually crease-less face and their pale-blue wings unfurl then fold neatly against their back as the concern diminishes from their blue eyes.

"Archangel Gabriel!" I exclaim, my heart filling with joy at seeing the androgynous face.

Archangel Gabriel slaps their hands against their cheeks. "Oh, thank the angels. I've finally found you."

I frown. "What do you mean?"

"I went to your farm. I've been worried about you, and Michael sent me to check on you. When you weren't there, I panicked. I've been searching for you for weeks." Their crystal-blue eyes flick from side to side, taking in the forest and the small clearing.

"Why?" I ask.

"After all the difficulties you've been through, I was worried. Worried for your mental health. Worried that you turned into a dragon again after Zacharias refused to see you for the umpteenth time. I wanted to make sure you were all right. When I found you were gone, I stressed."

I smile weakly. "I'm okay. I'm not happy, but I'm okay. I decided to look for my birth village, to see where my parents and I came from. I want to know what happened to them."

"Oh, sweetie. From what I heard happened to your parents, it sounds dangerous. You can't do that on your own."

"I have no one else to do it with. And besides, it's not like I don't have defense mechanisms and training from an expert warrior that I lived with for over a decade. Not to mention I can turn into a dragon." I grin. "I think it'll be fine."

The worry doesn't leave Archangel Gabriel's face. "I'm also worried about your mental health, sweetie. I don't want you to travel and do this alone. It sounds like it'll be an emotional ride."

When I don't look impressed, they continue, "I know you don't believe me, but things may not be as rosy as you might think."

I shake my head. "I don't think they'll be rosy. I'm

dying to get questions answered, so I'm going anyway."

Archangel Gabriel's shoulders sag. "Then I will have to come with you."

My jaw drops. "Whatever do you mean?"

Archangel Gabriel places a hand on their hip and waves a palm at me. "Like I said. I know you're capable of defending yourself physically, but I'm not sure you'll be able to handle it mentally. I'm worried about you without a shoulder to cry on. You've been through so much. You're tough, yes, but your heart and mind are in a very frail position. After everything you've done for the angels, I'm more than happy to help you and come with you. Besides, I'm sure the angels will need your help again soon. To reach you, they will need to know where you are."

I nod and lean my elbows on my knees. "Okay. It won't hurt to have some company. It's been quite lonesome for the last few weeks." I throw the last piece of bread into my mouth and chew while I study Archangel Gabriel from head to toe. They wear a powder-blue gown that flows down to their ankles, and their pale-blue wings spread wide and majestic. The face isn't quite masculine with its feminine edges. Their blue eyes are like a crystal spring and full of kindness, and their face is framed by blond wavy curls that fall to their shoulders. The attire is nothing like what the people of France wear in this day and age.

I swallow my mouthful. "On second thought, as much as I love your company and would love you to keep calling in to check on me from time to time, I think it's best if I do this one alone. I'm trying to be inconspicuous, and traveling with you will attract too much attention."

Archangel Gabriel's figure fades into particles then reforms as they change into a more current style of clothing. They lean on one hip, placing a hand on it with the palm facing out. "All right, sweetie. Is this better?"

I smile. "The clothing is better, but I think your mannerisms still give you away as being different. I think people will have too many questions about you everywhere I go. And besides, what am I supposed to tell them when they ask if you're male or female?"

A smile spreads across the archangel's face, and they lift an eyebrow. "I get your point, sweetie. I'll settle for calling in often. When I do, tell me if you want me to stay. You know I always will. I'll keep you company and make sure you're okay."

I grab their hand and smile, focusing on their eyes, finding comfort in the blue pureness of the crystal spring. "Thank you." I squeeze their hand.

"Oh, sweetie. Anytime." They lean forward and place a massive kiss on my cheek.

My smile spreads from ear to ear.

"Take care. Now that I know where you're heading, I'll visit soon. I'll tell Michael I know where you are." The creative archangel evaporates into particles then disappears.

CHAPTER FIVE

My vision fixes on the empty spot where Archangel Gabriel disappeared. A deep warmth fills my stomach. I feel so much better after the quick visit from the chirpy archangel. They are always cheerful and comforting. Zacharias would express his love and concern, but he has a completely different nature. He's a warrior. Just thinking about him brings a tear to my eye. I wipe it away with the back my hand and return my focus to Archangel Gabriel. It would be a shame to lose the lightheartedness that they brought in such a short period. I must focus on positivity to keep me stable, stopping me from being lost in my dragon form.

A pheasant lands in the clearing. I watch it for a few moments, studying its brown feathers. I'm ready to keep moving and walk to the center of the clearing. I grab my bag and throw it on my back. The sudden movement scares the pheasant away. Seeing this reminds me that flying would be the best form of travel to get me there quicker.

Removing the pin from my hair, I unclip it and watch it grow into the broomstick. A broad smile crosses my face. It's hard to be humble when admiring my handiwork. Straddling the broomstick, I head through the bushes, keeping low and out of sight. I fly several more hours, until midafternoon. The trees are thinning and giving me signs that I'm approaching another village. Remaining cautious, I dismount my broom and fold it away—the last thing I need is to expose myself as a witch.

The dry leaves crackle under my shoes as I weave my way through the trees. Different animal calls follow me, and I relish the sounds. A bird calls loudly from a tree above, and I glance up to see a tiny bluebird sitting on a branch. I'm surprised at how loud it calls for the size of the bird. While looking at it intently, I notice it's watching my every move. It calls loudly again. The sound almost seems like a warning call. This stirs something inside me, and my suspicions rise. Typically, if birds are scared, they fly away. They don't remain in view and call. About a minute later, another bluebird joins the first. They both seem to be watching me as I walk through the trees. I eye them with an equal amount of suspicion.

To an average human, birds acting like this would appear natural, but knowing what I can do, I suspect I may be looking at shape-shifters. These suspicions grow as I continue on my path. The birds seem to be following me and landing in each tree above or a few ahead of me. They hustle, fiddle, and fly around each other, yet at the same time, never take their eyes off me. They call loudly again, and a third bluebird arrives within a minute. It chirps loudly, watching and chatting with the others.

One stoops low, almost a swooping motion, then flies directly in front of me, circling then taking off, back up to the tree again. I can't tell if it's warning or welcoming, and I didn't want to shape-shift into the same form in case they were spying on me. The little birds continue to harass me with their actions until I approach a clearing in the trees and see signs of a village up ahead.

One bird flies toward the village and disappears around the corner of a building. Moments later, a man wearing simple medium-brown long pants and a light-brown jacket walks from that same spot heading in my direction. My heart beats faster as I watch his thin, lean form approach me. My edginess rises as I study him, but I'm unable to see any sign of a weapon. He is so tall, possibly about six feet, making my five feet and three inches feel extremely small. In the other villages I visited, I was never approached like this before. Something about this village is different.

He tosses his head, flicking his straight blond hair out of his green eyes, and focuses on me. The silence is pulling at my nerves, causing my stomach to churn. He is only a few feet away and observes me with a look that is far from comforting. I study his body language for any sign of aggression, but I can't tell. He seems neither friendly nor aggressive. It's neutral.

To ease the fluttering in my stomach, I break the silence. "Hello."

He pauses and stands with his legs apart and his arms crossed. Not the reaction I expect from a hello. After all, it isn't an unusual greeting when one first meets someone. Instead of calming the storm swirling in my stomach, it stirs up a mini tornado.

"Who are you? And what are you doing here?" He squints and observes me from head to toe, taking in the small backpack on my back. "A woman traveling alone is rare. You are either very powerful or extremely stupid."

My steps halt. I blink a few times as I process what he's not saying. His one comment gives me the indication that they don't take people at face value. Either I'm in danger, or I've finally stumbled into the right village. "Or perhaps I have no one to travel with," I propose, just to send him off course.

A slight flicker of doubt passes through his eyes, breaking into that confidence, but it's gone after a fleeting moment. "What are you doing in this area?"

By looking at him, I guess he's about ten years older than I am. "I'm looking for the village of Vezelay."

His eyes narrow. "Why are you looking for that village?"

"Because it's of interest to me."

"What is your interest?"

I mimic his stance and also cross my arms. "What business is it of yours?"

"If you don't tell me, you won't be permitted to go farther."

I huff then cock my hip to one side, my arms remaining crossed. People seem to think that they can push around a petite blond woman. If only they knew what's inside me. I'm sure they would have a change of heart if I transformed in front of them. The thought makes the corner of my mouth cock into a smile, which makes the man look more displeased. I push my mouth back to a flat line. "If you really must know, it's the place of my birth. I'm interested to see if I have long-lost family members there."

"Are your parents still there?"

I glare at him. "You really are one to ask a lot of questions without giving me any answers."

He raises an eyebrow. "I'm familiar with the village and want to know if I know your parents. That's all."

"If you must know, my parents are dead. They died when I was a young child. As I said, I've come to see if I have any lost family members."

His expression softens. "I'm sorry to hear that. What were your parents' names?"

"My father's name was Maurice Dragoo, and my mother's was Suzanne."

Recognition flashes through his green eyes, and they almost spark to life. "He was my uncle." The tall blond looks me over one more time. "That would make you my cousin. You're so tiny!" He reaches out an arm and hooks it around my shoulders. "Welcome, cousin. I'm sorry for the introduction, but we're wary of people around here. If you are Maurice Dragoo's daughter, you must be a shape-shifter as well."

I eye him questioningly. "What do you mean?"

"Your father was a shape-shifter. Didn't you know that?"

I decide it's best to play naive. I avoid the question. "I was very young when my father died."

A sadness crosses his face. "I wish you didn't have to go through that. Are you a shape-shifter?"

His eyes never leave my face as I glance at him, deciding how much I should reveal to him, before I slowly nod.

He smiles, and his eyes sparkle. "Welcome. You have arrived at Vezelay. We're not a typical village. That's why we're so cautious and why I bombarded you with questions. I'm Andre. What's your name?"

"Ava. Were you one of the bluebirds out in the forest?"

"Yes. I noticed that you were looking at us with suspicion. Normally humans just think we're animals and don't think anything of it."

"Well, I'm not just a human, and you were acting rather strange for a bluebird." I smile, taking in his features. I recognize a small resemblance between us, like the green eyes and blond hair. He has a thin frame but isn't petite like me.

We reach the edge of the village. "Come. Meet the rest of the family."

For the first time in a while, I smile sincerely. I'm happy right down to the bottom of my heart over a brighter future.

CHAPTER SIX

A s we walk toward the village, the two other bluebirds fly to the corner of the same building that Andre appeared from. Moments later, a male and female approach us while straightening their clothes.

The male's freckly face screws up, making him look almost angry as he eyes me with suspicion. Even under his blond hair, his complexion is pale, giving the impression that he never sees the sun.

"I guess you two heard our conversation," I say, eyeing them.

The woman doesn't look much older than I am. She pulls her long hair into a braid as she approaches. Her broad-necked dress flows loosely to the ground, covering her thin form with gathered material. "Of course, we heard you. That's what bird hearing is for."

My cousin gestures to the two approaching. "Ava, these are two members of the village, Henri and Yvonne. Despite the form we take, we aren't related."

Andre runs a hand through his blond hair as though almost embarrassed over the reception that the two approaching shape-shifters are giving me. He holds no hint of suspicion now that he knows we are related and I'm also a shape-shifter. He turns to the two acquaintances. "Ava is my cousin, in case you didn't hear that part."

Yvonne looks shocked. "Oh! We didn't hear that part."

She glances at Henri, and he shakes his head, answering her unasked question.

We enter the village, walking down the loosely cobbled street, passing several medium-sized cottages. Chickens run across the path and dig in the gardens.

"How many people live here?" I ask.

"There are roughly one hundred people, and we're all shape-shifters. It makes us a tight little community."

"I bet." A brown chicken digs at the corner of a cottage. It reminds me a lot of Mademoiselle, my childhood pet. "No wonder you were so protective on the outside, keeping an eye on me."

He chuckles. "Yes, it's nothing personal. We were merely keeping an eye on the village and protecting its inhabitants. Not everyone likes shape-shifters."

On the side of the street, people trade different food items without any stalls or passing money. The town seems to lack a commercial presence.

"Where are all the stands?"

Andre looks at me strangely. "What do you mean?"

I frown, confused over his question. I'm new to traveling outside my farm, but all the towns I passed through had stalls. Remembering that I'm still trying to make a good impression, I keep my voice even. "I mean, how do you buy your goods? Do you go to another village?" I start to think that maybe it's the shape-shifters' way to be naive about the world. Perhaps it's not just my experience of being sheltered by my guardians.

But then, as I look at my cousin, something seems to register in his mind.

"Oh, I understand. No, we don't have vendors here, but we do have money to spend in other villages when we need to get something we don't have in our village. That's rare, though, and only a few people go out of the village to shop. Occasionally, merchants will pass through."

My mouth lifts on one side. "And undoubtedly, you watch them like a hawk."

Andre smirks. "Or a bluebird."

Yvonne groans. "You'd think you'd learn some good humor for a change, Andre, especially while trying to make a good impression."

She rolls her eyes, and I chuckle. "Ah, it's all good. I'm related to him, apparently, so there's no escape for me."

"Lucky you." Sarcasm laces her voice. "I wouldn't be telling too many people that."

"I don't think I have to. I think he's going to tell everybody anyway. It's not like I have a choice."

We pass a few more cottages before Andre aims for

one. Its stone walls and slated roof stand broad and proud. Windows peer from the attic with a collection of small glass panes, matching the shuttered windows on the main house. Centered at the front of the house are open-shuttered doors, the top halves decorated with glass pieces that match the windows. On the right-hand side, a luscious vine covers a third of the stone wall with green foliage.

Andre opens the front door, indicating the three of us should enter. "This is my house."

In the center sits a young pregnant woman. Her blond hair is pulled tightly away from her face into a ponytail.

"Ava, this is my wife, Simonne."

My jaw drops, forgetting all niceties. "You're going to be a dad?"

"Yes, I am." His face beams with pride as he looks at his wife.

Simonne's face is expressionless. "And who is Ava?"

Andre's smile holds sincerity. "Ava is my cousin. She just arrived."

Simonne's eyes narrow, and she looks at me with suspicion.

A woman enters the room, holding a cup of something hot. "And how do you know?" Her shoulder-length blond hair falls over her slightly wrinkled face as she leans over, placing the cup on a table next to Simonne. Walking behind Simonne, she puts her hands on each shoulder of the pregnant lady and eyes me with a protective, almost canine, glare.

Simonne places her hand on top of the lady's. "Thanks, Mama."

Andre wrings his hands. It's almost like the combination of the two ladies puts him on edge. "It's okay, Marie. She's definitely my cousin. Look at her." He indicates my blond hair and green eyes.

"Yes. I can see the resemblance." Simonne's mother stares right at me. Her voice is rich with an underlying threat. "But blond hair and green eyes don't confirm they are from this village."

Andre's enthusiasm doesn't give. "She's Maurice Dragoo's daughter."

Simonne's expression remains distant as she looks at Andre then at her mother. "Is that the Maurice Dragoo who is dead?"

"Yes," a male answers from the doorway. Leaning against the frame to what looks like the kitchen behind him is a man of average height. What hair remains on his balding head is blond. His muscled body blocks only part of the entryway. He pushes off the doorframe and stands next to Simonne's mother. There is less hostility in his eyes than Marie's, yet his expression is not welcoming.

Andre sounds nervous as he introduces the two new people. "Ava, this is Gustave and Marie, Simonne's parents."

Despite the slightly hostile feeling I get from the two newcomers, I nod and attempt a smile. Gustave nods slightly, his face remaining expressionless.

Simonne's eyes narrow as they look at me then to Andre. "Wasn't their daughter killed too?"

Concern flicks across Andre's face, and the excitement is tainted. "They never found her body." He gazes at the man who had joined them. "Isn't that right, Gustave?"

The balding man shrugs, and some of the tension seems to lift from his frame. "That was the rumor. I guess you had to be there to know. Her body was never found."

"What do you think, Yvonne and Henri?" Marie's expression seems to hold some suspicion as she eyes me then looks at the two bluebird friends.

I don't blame her. If I thought someone was dead, I would be suspicious also.

Henri shrugs, and Yvonne looks lost.

"I don't know," the female bluebird says.

I attempt to ease some suspicion. "My father sent me off with his friend just before he was killed. He knew that I was in danger. His friend fled the area and lived on a secluded farm with his wife. They raised me like their own for many years."

"Who were these *friends* who raised you?" Marie accentuates the word *friends* and leans up against a wall.

Simonne stands and joins her, her pregnant belly sticking out prominently, and she crosses her arms over the mound.

"They were ordinary humans with big hearts and

43

open minds." I can feel my heartstrings pull as I mention my parents. I miss them fiercely.

Distain fills Marie's face, and I wonder if I said too much, but it's too late. "And where are these humans now?" Her mouth thins into a straight line.

It hurts me to have people talk about my guardians like that, and I can't hide it in my voice. "They are also dead."

Henri whistles. "Wow! It sounds like everybody you're associated with dies." He looks at Andre. "Are you sure it's safe to have her here?"

My cousin glares at his wife then frowns at Henri. "I'm sure it's as safe as having any other shape-shifter here. As you know, being a shape-shifter is risky business out in the real world."

"Yes, it is," Henri agrees. "But being around her seems to make life more dangerous. Even her father was killed, and he was a shape-shifter of great strength."

I was so young when my parents died. They had worked together to teach me things about my gifts. For some reason, I didn't know which one held which talent. They told me stories and gave me a dragon figurine to play with. I had suspicions that they were shape-shifters, but I couldn't understand why no one had mentioned my mother.

Since I'm exploring uncharted grounds, I decide to play it as safe as I can. "Was my father definitely a shape-shifter?"

Andre stares at me, mouth agape. "You mean, you don't know?"

"Well, naturally, because of my shape-shifting ability, I had my suspicions. I was never completely sure because I was so young when they died."

Simonne's eyes are accusing when she glares at me. "Then what do you know?"

"I just know that both my parents were killed. I assumed that at least one of them was a shape-shifter, but I was never sure. It's a small village. Perhaps you've also heard of my mother? Is her family here somewhere?"

The looks on the faces around me turn to shock, and a veil of silence drapes over us.

Finally, Gustave answers me. "Your mother wasn't a shape-shifter."

Purposefully, I drop my jaw. Simonne and her parents were cold to me before, but his tone reaches a whole new level, possibly even spiteful. I must tread as though I'm walking on eggshells. "You say that as though she was a dirty being. Was she human like my guardians, who you seem to despise even though you never met them?" A thousand thoughts run through my head. So far, no one has mentioned my witch heritage. Even though I know some of the information, I decide to continue as if naive. I don't know everything about my parents' past and the type of people they mixed with. Maybe the shape-shifters will be less bitter toward a person who is ignorant of their dishonorable heritage.

"No," Marie says harshly.

"Such a lighthearted conversation we're having for an introduction." Andre chuckles, a feeble attempt to break the tension. "We should focus on your father. He was a strong and robust shape-shifter, one that many shape-shifters looked up to."

"Until he broke the rules," Simonne snaps.

Andre's chuckle is tainted with tension. "That's what we hear, yes, but it's not what we know. You're way too young to know for sure, and you know how rumors fly in this little village."

I frown with confusion. Andre seems to be avoiding any unpleasantries, and Simonne and her parents are determined to hate me because of my parents. As much as I appreciate Andre's attempts to introduce me favorably, I need to know more about my parents, pleasant or not. "Why? What did he do?"

Andre sighs, a sign of his defeat. "He married your mother. That's all."

My jaw drops. "What's so bad about that?"

"Your mother was a witch." Marie lifts her chin and stands slightly before Simonne, almost in a protective gesture.

"She was a witch?" I gawk at Marie, simulating disbelief.

Marie glowers. "Yes. And we will do anything to keep people like her out of our village."

I gaze from Marie to Simonne, their posture hostile and unwelcoming. I take in Simonne's soft features and the plump roundness of the baby that's blooming. I can't believe that she and her parents are so heartless over this little fact. Simonne eyes me suspiciously.

"Is that a bad thing?" I ask, finding it difficult to understand the problem. "You say my father was dishonored because he married her. It sounds like it was just love. Why can't a witch and a shape-shifter marry?"

Simonne huffs and pushes off the wall she was leaning on, instantly flanked by both of her parents. "Witches and shape-shifters have been enemies for centuries. They must never marry each other."

Marie dismisses my lightheartedness. "If you are truly Suzanne's daughter, then you are also a witch."

I chuckle, trying to bring humor to my eyes. "No. I must've missed out on that gene." I playfully swipe a hand at her. "Only a simple shape-shifter here. What's the problem with my mother being a witch anyway? By your tone, it sounds like there's something wrong with that."

Marie moves protectively in front of Simonne again. "Witches persecute and kill shape-shifters, treating them like vermin."

I slap my hand over my mouth. This time the shock is real. "I had no idea. Humans raised me, and they didn't mention that to me. I haven't seen a witch or a shape-shifter since I was very young, before my parents were killed." I tap my mouth with my finger, thinking. "Although not all witches could be like that. It doesn't sound like my mom did that to my pop. Did you know my parents personally? Did you see how my mother treated shape-shifters?"

The disdainful look Marie gives me is priceless.

It takes all my effort not to smile. "Do you know how my parents were killed?" I gaze across at all three of them.

"We have no idea." Simonne rocks her weight to one leg. "Probably someone who hated them for being a witch and a shape-shifter married to each other." Her tone is distant as she says it.

Andre's eyes turn down, and he glances at me from the corner of them.

I face Yvonne and Henri. "Did you two know my parents?"

They both shake their head.

"You must remember, Ava, we were very young when it happened." Andre's voice is pained and sympathetic at the same time. "I remember bits of your father. He was a wonderful man. He was big and strong, nothing like you are in shape or size. He was one of the most revered shape-shifters in this village."

"Is there more than one shape-shifter village?" I ask.

"There are several." Yvonne sits on a stool in the corner of the room. "This is just one of many. We don't see the other villages very often."

I turn to Andre. "Why was my father so revered?"

His green eyes hold sadness as he looks at me. "He was one of our greatest warriors, a fierce protector of the village. His form was strong and robust. He was a great black bear." His eyes look hopeful. "Perhaps you picked up some of his genes despite your size. The fact that you survived for so long without any other contact with shape-shifters suggests you must have a strong form within you."

My head fills with images of strong animals. I need to think of one that I can tell him I am. From what I gather, it sounds as though they can only change into one form. "I guess you can say that." At the last second, my mind flashes back to the encounter Zacharias and I had in the forest. "I'm a wolf."

"That is an impressive form." Andre's eyes flick to his wife then to her parents.

I look at Simonne and indicate Henri and Yvonne. "I know these three are bluebirds. Strangely, they are all the same. What are you?"

She smirks at her husband, and it looks like a private joke passes between them, lightening her mood. In this one glimpse, my heart aches for Jehan, and I almost dive into that oblivion until she answers. "I am a fox."

"A fox!" I exclaim. "That's an interesting combination."

"Isn't it?" She chuckles. "I could eat him for breakfast. He better keep bringing the food in because I'm eating for two." She laughs, and we all join her.

"That's hilarious! Although I do hope it doesn't happen." I look sympathetically at my cousin. "Wow! Outranked by your wife."

The tension in the room seems to ease some more.

"Ha ha. It used to be a sore point but not so much

anymore." He chuckles. "At least I'm stronger than she is in human form."

"Does it bring you disgrace if you marry someone below your rank as an animal?" I ask.

Simonne shakes her head. "Of course not. We have a lot of strong females in our pack, and a lot of males would never breed if that were the case. We need the shape-shifter line to continue."

"Do the parents' shape-shifting genes conflict with or influence the children's shape-shifting genes?" I ask, looking at Simonne's parents. "Or does the animal come out randomly?"

Gustave leans lazily against the wall. "The animal often comes out randomly." He lifts his chin, looking proud. "Simonne followed our animals. My form is a wild dog, and Marie's is a fox."

"Just like Simonne?"

He nods. "Yes. Just like Simonne."

"Often, the animal is random. The strength of the animal carries through most of the time but not the actual shape." Yvonne crosses her legs.

The front door careens open, and a middle-aged man barges into the cottage, his face screwed up with displeasure. "There you are, Henri." He gazes around the room, and I notice a distinct slant to his eyes until they constrict when they land on Yvonne. "Why aren't you two at your post?" His voice booms through the small room, returning tension to the atmosphere.

Henri's face seems to turn paler. "We're getting Ava settled, Papa."

Confusion laces his face until his piercing eyes land on me. "And who is Ava?"

Andre clears his throat. "She's my cousin."

Henri's father huffs with a look of disinterest before he glowers at his son. "You and Yvonne have to be the worst guards of this village yet. A simple task for a bluebird to do, yet you can't even remain at your post."

Both Henri's and Yvonne's focus drops to the floor, and they clasp their hands in front of them.

"Get back out there!" Henri's father yells.

The two bluebirds hurry outside, leaving without saying a word. Henri's father follows them, slamming the door behind him.

The room falls into an awkward silence.

"He was rather grumpy," I say.

"He's in charge of the village's safety, and without any bluebirds on duty, we are left open for an invasion from unwanted visitors, like witches." Gustave crosses his arms over his chest.

Andre holds out his hand to me. "Come, cousin. Let's see my parents. They might be able to give you some more information, but you're welcome to stay with us for now." He makes eye contact with his wife, and she stiffly nods confirmation.

CHAPTER SEVEN

L eaving his wife, Simonne, and her parents behind, we exit Andre's cottage. It was a strange tension at Andre's house, and I'm glad to leave it behind. I get the feeling that I should have done more research into shape-shifters and witches before I came. But then, where would I find that kind of information? Ignorant seems the best way to act until I find out as much information as possible. I'm sure I'll be able to get away with more if I remain naive in the ways of the shape-shifting and witching world. It appears they will be more likely to forgive me or at least excuse me for being one or the other in the different colonies if I do.

The cobbled street between the farming cottages of Vezelay are thin, allowing the width of one cart to pass through at a time. Flowerbeds cluster in front of the cottages, their multicolored faces reaching proudly to the sky.

I stoop to rest the brilliant-red one in my palm,

cupping its beautiful, rounded petals. Releasing my grasp, I hurry to catch up with Andre and collide with someone. I gasp. "Oh. I'm sorry. I wasn't watching where I was going."

The woman smiles, creating a large dimple in one cheek and deepening the creases at the edge of her eyes. She pushes the end of her long sleeves to her elbows and flicks a long blond braid over her shoulder.

"Ava. This is Yvonne's mother, Jeanne." Andre hooks his arm with Jeanne's. "This is Ava, my cousin."

"Your cousin?" Uncertainty clouds Jeanne's face.

"Yes. She's Maurice and Suzanne's daughter."

The sweetness of her welcoming smile dampens in her eyes, yet her teeth still show. "How lovely. It's a shame I can't stay and chat. Maybe some other time."

It stings that so many of my own people have that same look when they find out who my parents were. I play along. "Sure. It's nice to meet you."

Jeanne's feet knock the loose stones, and her long blue skirt slaps against her legs as she hurries down the street.

Watching her leave, Andre says, "That's strange. She left in such a hurry. She must have something happening today." He extends his hooked arm to me. "Come. We can catch up with her later."

I loop my arm in his, and we head in the opposite direction as Jeanne.

"I'm sorry about the way my wife is acting." Andre looks ashamed. "Any association with witches is a risky business in this world. The feud has been going on for many generations and still burns bright. It's surprising that your mother was a witch and married a shape-shifter. Witches are more biased than shape-shifters, so she must have been one of a kind."

"I don't remember too much about my mother or father, to be honest. I was so young when they died that it's hard to remember. I know they were both good parents to me and loved me dearly. It was a great shock when my father told me to go with Piers and Caitline. I didn't know for quite some time that my parents had been murdered. My guardians held off telling me and only did after I demanded to go home because I missed my parents." I close my eyes, the ache of losing so many loved ones too painful. After a deep breath, I look at him. "My guardians didn't tell me anything about witches or shape-shifters or any of that, but if the war or the feud between the two is as bad as what you say, then I understand the suspicion."

"Just be ready. I don't know how my parents are going to act either. Perhaps they will also have a bias against witches and my uncle."

"I can handle their bias. Don't worry. I'm made of strong things. I can handle a lot, and I have been through a lot in this world."

"You had to have been through a lot if you've lost both your parents and your guardians. I'm sorry to hear life was so traumatic."

I nod in acknowledgment, trying to stay serene, yet my mind rushes to Zacharias and Jehan, two more people I've lost who are dear to my soul. I lost the love of my life forever and my guardian angel indefinitely after he was cursed to be earthbound. Both of them were taken from me on the same day. But these are things I cannot explain to my cousin. He probably knows nothing of the angelic world. And how do I explain that a demon killed my husband and soul mate? No, that I must keep silent for now.

We walk through the small village until we near the end of the houses. Andre turns sharply toward one of the houses at the end of the road. It is quaint, nothing flashy, just like the rest of the village. Wheat fields stretch out behind it, reminding me of my childhood. Andre cracks open the door slightly, and calls, "Hello, Mama and Papa."

"Son. Come in," a man calls from inside the house.

Andre enters, motioning for me to come.

"What are you doing here? I thought it was your turn on guard duty," the man calls before he comes around the corner. He hitches up his long brown pants then tugs at the front of his button-up dark-blue jacket. He halts when his eyes fall on me.

"Hello, Papa. Yes, I am on guard duty today. This is who I picked up." Andre tilts his head toward me.

His father studies me, and a strange look crosses his round face. "Who is she?"

"Ava, this is my father, Theodore. Papa, this is your niece. She is Maurice Dragoo's daughter."

A deep frown wrinkles his forehead, and he roughs his brown beret, tousling his curly blond hair. "Are you sure? How do you know?"

"Because as she approached our town, I spotted her, and she recognized me as a shape-shifter even though I was in my bluebird form. When I changed and approached her, she said she was looking for information about her parents and her upbringing." When his father's frown deepens, he adds, "She mentioned them by name."

His father studies me some more, a strange expression in his eyes. "I do see the resemblance, but we thought you died too."

"I seem to be getting that a lot." I smile wanly. "I had no idea I was supposed to be dead. That would explain why none of my family came looking for me."

A woman emerges around the corner of the room. Her ample hips sway the fabric of her long blue dress. She walks straight to me and places a hand on my cheek. Her blue eyes cloud with compassion. "Oh, my dear. I just heard. I'm Rosa, your aunt. If we'd known you were alive, we would have looked for you. We had no idea." A strand of blond hair falls loose from her plait, and she hooks it behind her ear. "They never found your body, but your parents were made into such a mess that we assumed you were lost in it."

I haven't heard any details of my parents' death, and her statement makes me picture a horrific scene. My heart feels heavy, and images of Jehan and my guardian parents' deaths flash into my mind. These flashbacks to my loved ones are happening too often, making it hard to move on. To hide my pain, I drop my eyes to the ground. "I'm starting to think my parents' death was worse than I thought."

"It was messy." Theodore rubs his long blue sleeve and looks to the corner of the room. "I wish I could tell you otherwise." He gazes at Andre. "Has she been told why we think her parents were killed?"

Andre nods, sadness filling his face.

Theodore's eyes seem to narrow as he looks at me. "Do we need to worry about you being a witch as well?"

I feign shock and make sure I stare directly into his eyes. "What makes you think I would be a witch?"

His scrutinizing gaze doesn't falter. "Because your mother was a witch. That gene is strong. It travels well through the woman's genes and onto her daughters."

"Papa!" Andre exclaims then looks at me apologetically.

My uncle changes his tone slightly. "Or so I have heard."

I work hard on keeping a straight face. "Well, I have definitely not seen any sign of a witch in my blood. Although I can confirm that I'm a shape-shifter."

One blond eyebrow lifts as Theodore observes me closely. "Really? What form do you hold?"

"I'm a wolf." I lift my chin slightly. After having the conversation with Andre's friends and wife, I know it's a form to be proud of.

Theodore's and Rosa's eyes widen. "I see you've inherited your father's gene and become a strong shape-shifter."

I maintain my air of naivete. "If you class the wolf as a strong animal, then I have inherited my father's gene of being a strong shape-shifter, but as for my mother's gene, I haven't seen anything that indicates me being a witch."

"Then that's good for you," Theodore answers, and I can't tell if he believes me or not. "It's much safer for you to be only a shape-shifter in this village. We heard that when your parents were killed, the killers were also after you. They believed that you were half and half because you were born from both a shape-shifter and a witch." Theodore glances at Rosa. "As Rosa said, there was so much blood everywhere, we assumed they had killed you as well as your parents—and that they had gone through your parents to get to you." His scrutinizing glare returns to me. "Obviously, they were wrong in assuming that you're half witch and half shape-shifter."

I chuckle, doing my best to sound innocent. "Oh, they were so wrong. I wouldn't have a clue how to cast a spell. Surely, I would know if something like that exists inside of me, wouldn't I?" A churning fills my stomach, and I can feel my blood warming. The dragon longs to break free and teach these bigots a thing or two. Instead of allowing my emotions to take over, I take deep breaths, working hard to make them seem natural as I execute my witch powers to tame the beast inside of me. If only I could tell them that it's the witch in me that's keeping them alive right now.

Rosa must read something in my expression, for her

blue eyes flash with worry, and she rubs my upper arm. "Yes, that's right. You're over the age of twenty-one, so you would certainly know by now." She smiles sweetly. "Come, you must be hungry. You must have traveled far." She leads me by the arm to the dining room table.

My stomach growls at the mention of food. "Yes, I am. Thank you, that would be lovely. I've been on the road for weeks, and all I've eaten is dried fruit, nuts, and very little else."

Rosa prepares homemade bread, eggs, and beans for me. The food is plain yet delicious. Anything different than dried fruit and nuts is a godsend.

I sense I'm being watched and turn to find my uncle leaning against the wall and staring at me, his expression unreadable. I swallow my mouthful, my throat struggling over the unchewed portion. I'm not sure how to take his staring, but something tells me I need to watch every action I make in this village. So far, the reception has been confusing and contradictive. I tear off another clump of bread, observing my uncle as openly as he's watching me. He realizes what I'm doing, and his expression changes.

He clears his throat and pushes off the wall to stand straight. "It's great to have you back. I had no idea you were still alive, but it's good to see that you're well." He clasps his hands in front of himself. "Sorry I'm staring at you. I'm just shocked to see you alive, when we had no idea all this time."

I nod as I finish my mouthful of food. "That's okay. I understand. I can't say that I wouldn't have liked to live and grow up in this village. It would have been nice to have other children my age to play with, but I had excellent guardians. They looked after me very well."

He smiles. "Then you fell into some good luck."

I shrug. "I wouldn't call it luck. Apparently, my papa was friends with them beforehand." I purposefully leave out that my guardians were humans. I have a hunch that this will stir up emotions, as it did with Simonne and her parents.

"Oh!" A strange look crosses his face.

I attempt to bring the conversation away from my upbringing. "Andre brought me here because he thought you might be able to enlighten me a little more about my parents and what they did. I'm eager to know."

His face fills with a broad smile. "I loved my brother. I begged him not to marry the witch. I knew it would only bring trouble, and it was hard to accept that I would be related to a witch. They have been the source of so much trouble for our village."

"What do you mean?"

He takes a deep breath, as though pushing aside an unpleasant feeling. "So many of our members have disappeared. Often, we find out later that they were kidnapped by witches and persecuted. Very few return." His eyes sharpen. "I hope you understand that when your father decided to marry your mother, it wasn't accepted in the village."

I want to scream at him that I don't understand their

bias. Instead, I nod respectfully. "It's a shame to hear that this is the way it is. I'm sorry this village went through that." I push my mostly empty plate aside. "But I don't remember my mother being anything like that. I only remember the love that poured out of her into me. I don't remember her with the rest of the villagers, but I'm sure there was some kind of animosity."

"You have no idea," he grumbles.

"Even though she treated shape-shifters the same as anyone else?"

"That doesn't matter. Your mother was a witch." He thumped his fist on the table.

"But shouldn't you treat others the way they treat you? It doesn't make sense to treat a witch who is friendly to shape-shifters the same as witches who persecute shape-shifters. I'm sure my mom didn't cause harm to any shape-shifters."

"It doesn't make any difference. Even though your mother never did anything wrong to anybody in the village, there was constant hostility toward her, as there should have been," Rosa says. Her blue eyes burn with a strange emotion I can't decipher. "She was a witch, and none of the shape-shifters would put up with her presence in our town. No one knew when she would decide to change her ways and treat us like the other witches treated us. Because of this, they moved to a little hut outside of town, on its own. As far as I know, hardly anyone knew where they lived. Whether it was a good or bad move, I do not know. In any case, their marriage still led to their deaths. Neither side saw it as favorable."

"And how did you relate to my father?" I ask Theodore.

"I loved my brother, but I couldn't support him publicly." His expression looks torn, as though begging for understanding. "I had to cut him out of my life. It was a tough decision to make, one I wish I could turn back and make again."

"My father was a bear shape-shifter. If the strength of the genes of the animal runs through the family, what's your shape-shifting form?" I frown, trying to get my head around the theory. I shrug and spread my arms wide. "When your son is a bluebird."

His eyes dart to Andre. "The strength of the animal does not always flow through the genes. My brother was a strong shape-shifting animal. Unfortunately, I ended up with something much less."

"Which is?" I ask.

"I turn into a hawk." He almost looks shameful at the admission, even though he wouldn't have had a choice.

I weigh all the emotions that this would have brought to him and his family. "Wouldn't this have caused some resentment between you and my father?"

He shrugs and tilts his head to the side. "Sure. I'd be lying if I said I wasn't jealous of his strong form, but a hawk also has its advantages. So, I'm happy with my shape-shifting form. I just didn't receive the glory that my brother did. Although, let me tell you, don't mess with a hawk." He levels his eyes at me.

"I'll keep that in mind." I smile wryly as I study his face. I can tell he's serious, but in comparison, it's nothing to my forms, even my wolf form, which I've admitted to.

CHAPTER EIGHT

A ndre and I walk back to his place, and I can't help but think that there must've been betrayal along the way. It seems a little strange that Mom and Pop would live in such a secluded place that hardly anyone knew about, yet they still ended up murdered. They must have moved to protect themselves and hide from the criticism and hostility, making sure hardly anyone knew their location. So, the only way to make sense of their murder is if someone betrayed them. Possibly they fell upon bad luck and someone stumbled across their little cottage and killed them. But the circumstances surrounding their murders and that I was sent away with Pop's best friend brings my thoughts back around to the option of betrayal. I can't help but think about my uncle's hawk form and how he made sure he mentioned that a hawk shouldn't be messed with. What exactly did he mean by that? Was that a warning? Of course, I know that a hawk isn't a useless bird. They are fierce predators. My uncle and aunt weren't overly friendly to me. I frown. Maybe I'm reading too much into it.

We're halfway to Andre's house when he mentions, "You're very quiet."

"Sorry. I have a lot on my mind. It's stirring up a lot of emotions." I give him a sad smile.

"Can I do anything to help?"

I shake my head. "No, I don't think so. I'm just trying to think things through."

We walk a few more steps in silence.

"I know my father wasn't that helpful with information. I hope you got a little bit out of that."

I nod. "I think so." My forehead creases. "Does anyone know who killed them?"

His eyes are apologetic as he shakes his head. "No. I don't think so. Not that I know of. It certainly wasn't announced if they found out who killed them."

"Didn't anybody investigate what happened to them?"

"I'm sorry. I was so young. I don't know anything about it. It would be a question you would have to ask the parents."

I nod, but deep down, I think that's going to be a dead end. "Thanks for taking me there."

"No problem. If you have any more questions, we can go back later. Maybe another day. Perhaps my father will be more giving of information after he gets over the shock that you're alive. Don't worry too much about his comment about him being a hawk and not to take them for granted. I honestly think he has not-so-important-animal syndrome." He eyes me from head to toe. "Judging by your size, I would say you know what that is, but I'm not too sure." He studies my face as though looking for a reaction. "You seem to be quite strong in nature and not worried or put off about your size."

I smirk at him, just holding back a laugh. If only they knew what I really am or could be. "No. I don't have small person syndrome."

He nods, seeming to accept my statement. "You seem to have an inner strength that wouldn't allow you to put yourself down about your size."

I nudge him with my elbow and peer at him under a raised eyebrow. "Ahh. An observant type."

He smirks. "How do you think I stay alive while being married to a fox?"

"Yes, that would be a tricky situation at times, especially if she's upset with you."

We reach his home and enter, following the clattering sound to the kitchen. Simonne's shoulders stiffen as we enter, and the atmosphere in the room turns icy as her eyes land on me. For a moment, I watch the struggle on her face as she pushes the iciness away, replacing it with something warmer. I hope it's just her pregnancy hormones protesting, not her real personality.

"Are your parents gone?" Andre asks.

She nods then smiles, the expression not reflected in

her eyes. "So, how'd it go? Did you learn anything new or find out anything useful?"

Andre shakes his head. "I don't think Papa was that useful, but perhaps it helped." He turns and looks at me for confirmation.

Attempting to be reassuring, I smile. "I think it helped a little, although I still have a lot of questions on my mind. Hopefully, time should uncover the answers." A breeze from the window carries a delicious smell in my direction, and my stomach growls. I look around the kitchen, trying to find the source. "What's cooking?" I take in an exaggerated breath. "It smells delicious."

"I've roasted a pheasant and baked some vegetables in the oven. I hope you like it." The look she shoots my way challenges me to disagree.

I smile. "If it tastes anything like it smells, it'll be delicious." I know I've said the right thing when her face softens.

Andre places an arm around Simonne's shoulders. "Don't worry. She's an excellent cook. How do you think I got this belly?" He pushes out his abdomen and taps it. "It makes it so hard to change into a tiny bird when I've put on so much weight."

I laugh at his nonexistent belly. "I was wondering how you manage to turn into such a small form." I think about my wolf and how it's quite a substantial form. "I have enough trouble turning myself into a wolf. It's quite a stretch at times."

"Turning into a fox is also hard. It's much smaller than I am, even though I'm not that big." Simonne rubs her baby bump. "But there are people who change into forms that are much different from them, including my husband. Although I must say, he is one of the extremes." She grabs plates out of the cupboard and places them on the kitchen bench. "Anyway, it's time to eat." She spreads the plates and starts loading them with the carved pheasant and roasted vegetables, then places a hunk of bread on the side.

After taking the plate she hands me, I sit at the table.

I cut off a piece of pheasant and place it in my mouth. I almost groan over the flavor, especially after such a long trip with only travel food. The food Rosa served me was nice and broke some of my hunger, but the divine smell of Simonne's meal is nothing compared to its taste.

"This is delicious." I take in another morsel and chew it slowly, savoring the delightful flavors. "It's been so long since I've had a decent meal, and this is a lot nicer than I've tasted in a very long time."

She looks surprised. "Don't you cook for yourself?"

I'm about to answer when I think of Jehan and how he used to make my dinners. A tear tumbles down my cheek. I wipe it away with my sleeve. My lips pucker as I try to stop the tears from falling.

Simonne's face is troubled. "Oh, I'm sorry. Did I say something wrong?"

I shake my head. "I recently lost my husband. He was murdered. It was such a horrible, traumatic experience. I haven't been thinking about myself since then. It suddenly dawned on me that he used to do all the cooking. I was always tending to the farm." When I see her frown, I explain. "We preferred it that way."

She forces a smile. "Oh, I'm so sorry. It's strange that your husband used to cook for you."

"He was creative. His family used to make handmade bags and sell them at the markets. He liked to cook. I would help him make the bags, but I would also tend the farm. I loved the connection with animals. I guess it's a shape-shifter thing." I smile weakly.

"Was he a shape-shifter?" Andre asks.

"No. He was human."

Simonne looks shocked. "Did he know about you being a shape-shifter?"

I nod. "Yes. He was an open-minded human, and I loved him dearly." I look up and see repugnance on her face. "Is that also forbidden?"

"Yes, it is." A chilliness enters her voice.

"I had no idea," I say with an innocence I don't hold. I may have lived a sheltered life, but it doesn't take much to understand that a shape-shifter and a human shouldn't mix, let alone marry.

"I'm sure you didn't." She smiles wryly. The iciness in her voice remains. "You seem to be completely ignorant of our ways."

"She can't help it, can she?" Andre comes to my defense. "It's not like she's been raised with us. Humans raised her. What else would she know?" He sounds annoyed with his wife.

She glares at him. "Oh, stop your chirping, bluebird."

His expression turns cold until, a few moments later, laughter bursts from her mouth. I look at her in surprise.

Simonne reaches across the table and places a hand on my arm. "I'm sorry. My pregnancy hormones must be getting to me. Of course, you didn't know. You wouldn't know any different." She turns to her husband. "And sorry, darling. I'm getting cranky in the last part of my pregnancy."

He nods enthusiastically, agreeing with her whole-heartedly.

Holding my silence, I continue eating my dinner, savoring every mouthful. I'm not about to let the delicious food go to waste, despite the company. It's been a long time since I've eaten a decent meal. When I'm done, I wait in awkward silence until Andre and Simonne finish, twiddling my thumbs under the table.

When they set their silverware down, I grab their plates and head to the bucket on the bench. "I'll do the washing up. It's the least I can do."

Andre pushes his chair back from the table, a horrified look on his face.

I wave a hand at him, indicating for him to remain seated. "No, honestly, it used to be my job after my husband cooked. I'm happy to wash the dishes." As I wipe the dirty plates with the soapy water, I have to hide the smirk that creeps onto my face. Naturally, I leave out the part that I used to do the dishes with magic. This time there will be no magic involved. I'll be doing them the human way—slowly by hand—anything to get out of the awkward conversation.

Andre brings out some blankets and places them neatly in the corner on the floor. He looks at me apologetically. "We don't have an extra room, but you can sleep on the couch. Make yourself comfortable in this corner here."

I smile at him. He's growing on me. "Thank you. That's more than enough."

"You're welcome to stay as long as you need if you can put up with my wife's moodiness. I'm afraid the late stages of pregnancy are starting to affect her personality. Don't tell her I said that, though." A sheepish look covers his face.

"We all get a little moody sometimes. It's just nice to be near family again. After my husband passed away, I needed to find someone to connect with. He was everything I had on this earth."

"I understand. You're welcome to stay here. I think we would get along." He leaves me, entering the room where Simonne is already preparing for bed.

I finish the dishes, head over to the corner, and lie on the couch. I wriggle and turn, trying to settle into the softness of the blanket without success. Something tells me that even if it were the most luxurious bed in the world, I wouldn't sleep well tonight anyway. My mind buzzes with information and thoughts. I command my body to be still, only to be ignored.

I give up on sleep when I hear the soft breaths

deepen in the other room. I flick the blanket aside and open the door, sneaking quietly outside and shutting it without a click. I need to catch some fresh air.

The moon is almost full, casting dark shadows in all directions and adding an eerie light to the atmosphere. My nerves fire, putting me on edge, but I welcome the open space. I've been so used to traveling and living out in the open for the last few weeks that it holds a comforting feeling even with the eerie shadows.

I pace slowly around the outside of the house, running my hands down my clothes to straighten them, more out of habit than anything else, as my mind remains deep in thought. The knowledge of my parents' murder isn't new, but I hadn't realized an entire community was against them and their relationship. I used to believe they were killed because they'd annoyed someone or were too powerful, not because of the simple reason that they were a shape-shifter and a witch who'd married and had a child.

Piers and Caitline hadn't told me I was in danger as well. I didn't know that whoever had killed my parents wanted to kill me, too, and that I wasn't meant to survive. The reason for Zacharias's arrival on our farm when I was a child is starting to become clearer. He wasn't there just to protect me from demons but from my past and people who didn't like shape-shifters and witches. I'll have to remain alert, even though I lied about my witch legacy. I must hide it from these people. I don't know if the murderer or murderers are still alive and if they know who I am. I'm sure the word will travel fast in this little village. The mere thought of it puts me on edge again. Trying to calm my nerves, I take in deep breaths as I wander around the yard.

Something catches my eye.

"Ava." The sharp voice startles me, and I turn in the direction of the movement.

CHAPTER NINE

Instinctively I shape-shift, remembering at the last second what animal form I said I change into. I've spent so much time as a dragon since Jehan's death, but I manage to turn into a wolf at the last split second. I land on all fours and growl until my eyes focus on who called me.

Standing before me with an amused look on their face is Archangel Gabriel. The androgynous angel's pale-blue wings and sky-blue gown, illuminated by the moonlight, almost make them look like a cloud in the night. Their soft face is clear to me with my wolf sight.

They cock a hand at me. "Oh, sweetie. Did I startle you? I'm sorry." Except I could see on the archangel's face that they weren't that sorry. The crystal-blue eyes study my form, and they smirk. "That's an interesting choice when I know you could be something far more vicious."

Knowing the friendly archangel is right and feeling

slightly embarrassed, I change back into my human form and bend down to pick up my clothes, pulling them back on over my shape-shifting underwear. "Archangel Gabriel, it's a pleasant surprise. I wasn't expecting you so soon."

"Oh, sweetie. It's not soon. It's been quite a while since I last saw you. You seem on edge. I hope all is going well."

I lower my voice and survey the area for any villagers. With the coast clear, my shoulders relax. "Not great, but good enough that I can handle it. I've only just arrived, and I have a lot to sort through."

Sadness washes over their face. "I'm sorry to hear that, but right now, we need you, which is why I've called. The gatekeeper is causing mischief again, and we need your help."

"I'll do anything to help you against the gatekeeper." I hold out my arm. "Let's go."

Archangel Gabriel grabs me with a dainty hand, and I feel my particles being pulled apart and maneuvering as we teleport. The second we land, my body reforms and shapes into a dragon. My sight and my color coordination change, and I pause to look around.

My eyes land on the gatekeeper in the distance. A tattered white body wrap hangs limply from his scrawny form, ending at the knee, showing off his dry, cracked bare feet. He shuffles a few feet closer holding his staff, which stands taller than his small form. The bandage remains wrapped around his head, even after all these centuries. It covers a wound that continues to weep, serving as a constant reminder of the being that caused him pain. Zacharias filled me in about the accident, an innocent mistake by Zacharias and Archangel Michael that left the creepy gatekeeper with only one eye.

That one eye fixes on me, and a smug look crosses his face. Oh, how I long to wipe that look away. I push off the ground and flap my expansive dragon wings. Their green brilliance folds in front of me and then up behind me. They lift me higher and higher as I aim toward the gatekeeper and his demonic minions pouring from the gatekeeper's portal. He isn't that far away, but I know he will soon disappear into the portal, and I won't be able to catch him. Maybe one day I'll be able to get to him in time and get revenge for Jehan and Zacharias, enabling Zacharias to live a normal life again. From what I've heard, the angels still haven't found his wings. They speculate that the wings are being kept as a trophy in one of the gatekeeper's lairs.

This thought causes me to glower, bunching the scales on my forehead. I flap my wings with enormous effort, and the distance to the gatekeeper disappears with each movement. Just as I feared, the slimy gatekeeper moves toward the entrance of his portal when I'm still too far away to breathe fire at him.

I flap faster, trying profusely to get to him. The deep sensation of burning fills my stomach, and I let it whirl and build as it churns like a furnace ready to spew forth in a plume of fire. The second I think I have a chance, I release its vengeance, hoping it will lap at the gatekeeper's ankles as he runs through the portal, escaping the coward's way, like he usually does, but I know I'm just a few seconds too late as the portal closes down on itself and disappears.

In frustration, I spew the large, angry flames at several demons that remain and watch with little satisfaction as their bodies turn into dust and dissipate to the earth.

The frustration burns long and deep inside my stomach, building more, ready to be propelled. Spotting a new target, I set it free, aiming at more of the demons left behind. They burn, and their bodies turn to dust.

After I've scorched the majority of the demons in this area, I maneuver slowly in the other direction and take to the war field. I don't know where we are, but it's clear that a large number of demons are overtaking the area.

In the distance, I spot Gabriel throwing their shuriken while standing not far from Archangel Michael—a position that was once Zacharias's. It's a place of pride and joy in the duty of protecting the great Archangel Michael. Michael's sapphire-blue eyes land on me, and I can see that he's thrilled I've arrived. He must not have expected me to come after everything I'd been through. Despite Zacharias cutting me from his life and the death of Jehan, my involvement with the angels isn't finished. I'm not going to give up now. I have a score to settle with the gatekeeper and his minions. It won't bring Jehan back, but it could help

Zacharias, enabling him to return to his duty and perhaps even mend our relationship.

I spot a demon sneaking up behind Archangel Michael. Its bat-like wings spread wide, and it poises its hand with its palm out, ready to throw its pulses of demonic power into the archangel. The pulses have the potential to weaken angels or maim them, and when weakened, they're left vulnerable to being abducted, as Michael was before. It was one of the draw cards that led to Zacharias's downfall. Despite the danger he knew he was facing, Zacharias was loyal to the depth of his bones.

I increase my speed, drawing large amounts of power, and jump over Archangel Michael. I shoot a plume of fire straight onto the demon about to attack the leader of the archangels. The demon stumbles and falls to its knees, shooting black pulses in the same instant, aiming directly at me. It hits me full in the stomach, and I roar in agony. My flight waivers, yet the pulse doesn't bring me down. Instead, it makes me more determined to catch them and knock them down.

I breathe my fire over the demon and watch the beast disintegrate. The specks of dust float slowly to the ground, the demon no longer a threat. Michael's praise rises to my ears. He is the reason Zacharias was my guardian. He believed I was worth saving, and now he beams at me with pride.

I do my rounds of the battlefield, taking in the unfair advantage that the demons have in numbers compared to the angels. I know what I must do. Approaching a group of demons a safe distance from the angels, I douse them in a plume of fire, disintegrating them. I continue this until the numbers are in the angels' favor, and the demons lose their assurance. I then land amidst the angels.

Michael calls, "Thank you, Ava. I'm so glad to have you back to normal again. We definitely needed your help."

I change back into my human form. "I'm always happy to help, Archangel Michael. You know that."

He smiles briefly. "How have you been holding up?"

I look at the ground. "I'm better now. Not great, but I'm better than before. I seem to have lost everybody who is dear to me in life."

"Gabriel said you're seeing your extended family."

"Yes, but I'm not sure how that's going. Only time will tell. It's my first day there, and already I feel as though there are a lot of suspicions. I have a lot of work to do to fit into my old family. I'll see how it goes. They are anti-witch, and as you know, that could be a problem for me."

Archangel Michael walks forward and places a hand on my shoulder. "Let us know if there's anything we can do. You're like family to us, even though you're not an angel. I believe Gabriel will be keen to drop in on you and see how you're doing."

Gabriel confirms with enthusiasm, "Absolutely. I can't wait to keep in contact with her and watch over her. I've already called a few times, haven't I, sweetie?" They turn to me.

"Yes, you have. But remember, I'm not a little girl anymore, and I have many defenses I can use to protect myself." I smirk. "After all, you're the ones calling on me to help out these days, but I love your affectionate visits."

Archangel Gabriel places an arm over my shoulders. "Well, I'll be doing a lot more of those, sweetie."

I smile up at them and step back to hold out my hand. "Right now, I need to get back before they realize I'm gone. That will only raise more suspicions. I'm already under fire from my cousin's wife, and perhaps even their parents." I turn to Archangel Michael. "I'll keep you updated with Gabriel's visits."

Gabriel grabs my hand, and instantly I feel my particles dissipating then reforming as we land back in town.

CHAPTER TEN

Archangel Gabriel delivers me to the house, and something unusual catches my eye. A small light flickers in the window. I gaze at the archangel, worry gripping my soul.

"What is it, sweetie?"

"There's light shining from the window of the house. That wasn't on before."

They observe the house, their peaceful face furrowing into a frown. "Do you need me to stick around?"

I shake my head. "No. I'll handle it."

The archangel embraces me and whispers in my ear, "All right, but don't scare them too much with the dragon." Releasing me from the hug, they wink then dissipate, leaving me standing alone.

Despite knowing I have special powers and unique defense mechanisms with my different shapes and my witch abilities, I can't help but feel nervous. I came here to make connections with my family. I want to find people I can fit in with and somewhere I can call my home. It seems strange, but this is important to me. I hold on to the hope that if I meet a whole village or family that cares for me, and I for them, I won't lose everyone I care about again. That way, I'll always have someone to rely on. That makes it essential for me to gain the trust of the people living in the house where I'm staying.

I think about turning invisible and reappearing in my bed. Then I think better of it. Perhaps the person is already in the living room and has seen my bed empty. That's something I'll never be able to explain. Instead, I take a deep breath, slowly pull the door handle down, and enter the room. My heart pumps loudly, protesting inside my rib cage over my anxiousness. Filling my lungs with air, I attempt to slow my heartbeat, repeating the process with several more deep breaths. I can feel myself starting to calm and become level-headed until my eyes land on the flickering candle in the hand that holds it.

"Simonne!" All my effort to calm myself vanishes.

Her eyes narrow, full of suspicion, and her face looks eerie in the flickering shadows of the candlelight. "Ava." Her neutral voice betrays the icy emotions I can see in her eyes.

Seeing in her eyes that she has already convicted me, I work on my defense. "I was just taking a walk. I couldn't sleep." I shrug.

She lifts an eyebrow. "In the middle of the night?"

"Yes. I don't see why not. I've been living outdoors while I've been traveling. I'm not used to being inside all the time." Sticking close to the truth is the best option.

She eyes me from head to toe. "I thought I heard voices."

"I'm sorry if I disturbed you. Did I wake you?"

"No. I had to go to the bathroom. One of the many faults of being this pregnant and having a baby sitting on your bladder."

I curse myself inwardly. I didn't think of that when I snuck out. Having never been pregnant, I hadn't realized what it would do to the body and how often it would wake someone during the night. "That must be uncomfortable." Even though she said I hadn't, I repeat, "I'm sorry if I woke you. I merely wanted some fresh air."

Her eyes sharpen, and her lips push out suspiciously. "I swear I heard you talking to someone. Who's out there?"

I gaze directly into her eyes. "No one. I was chatting to myself. I'm sorry. I guess it's a habit I picked up from traveling without companionship."

She lifts her chin and looks down at me, a feat she didn't need to do, considering my shortness. "You're acting rather strange for a shape-shifter. Perhaps you should check out the other side of your family as well, you know, the witching side. You may find you relate to them more." Her eyes are like sharp knives, piercing down at me.

I know she means this to be an insult, but I don't take it that way. Deep down, I know that she's partly right, though I haven't met the witches, and the shape-shifters haven't said anything nice about them.

I rub my arm while deep in thought. "Didn't you say the witches persecute the shape-shifters?"

"Yes, they do." She looks smug, and it saddens me more than anything.

"I haven't attempted to hurt anyone in this village in any way."

"But perhaps you have a dominant part of a witch lying within you, yet to wake. Maybe you need to discover if they are part of your family more than we are."

It's evident as I stare at Simonne that it's going to take a lot for her to like me. "Have I done something to offend you?" I ask.

"You offended me when you were born. Something that is half shape-shifter and half witch is an abomination and should be killed at birth."

Even though I suspected that was her belief, it slaps me across the face when she says the words—having them spoken out loud drills it in farther. She's probably letting her animosity pour right out now that Andre isn't near.

"Don't hold back your thoughts." I let some spite shine through my voice. "A person can't help how they're born. Each person has a soul that's just as valuable as the next. They don't have a say about what blood runs through their veins. It shouldn't determine how they're judged."

"That's your opinion, not mine." She pulls the shawl tighter around her shoulders. "Well, now that you're back, I'm returning to bed." She turns abruptly, taking the light and the iciness with her.

Yanking my shawl from my shoulders, I throw it down. I must remember Simonne's disturbed sleep patterns in the future. After tonight, I get the feeling she doesn't like me and would do anything to try and put me on display, shaming me in front of the rest of the village. My attempt to catch a short sleep before dawn is unsuccessful. It seems like my head hits the couch for only a few minutes before the sunlight shines through the window.

I sit and ponder what to do as I wait for the rest of the household to wake. My witching powers itch at the restricted edges, burning to be used, but I'm not game to use them in case I'm discovered.

I ponder what Simonne said. Perhaps it's a good idea to visit my witch side as well and investigate to see how they act and what my family members are like there. Maybe my parents' betrayal came from the witches. As the sun shines brighter within the house, I start to pack my things into my tiny bag.

"What are you doing?" Andre stands in his bedroom doorway. His hair is disheveled, and he wipes the sleep from his eyes as if he can't believe what he's seeing.

"I think I should go visit the other side of my family as well."

He blinks in disbelief. "The witches?"

"Yes, the witches."

"That's absurd."

I let out a pent-up breath. "It may be a good idea. I may find out who betrayed my parents."

"Yeah, and they'll probably kill you in the process or kill you before you can find out. You're a shape-shifter. They're going to know it or find out at some stage. I haven't met one shape-shifter who's gone near the witches and come back alive."

"I am made of tough things."

He smirks. "Yeah, you're a wolf. I get that. Your father was a bear, and they still murdered him. They have powers we can't contend with."

I smile. I know he's only trying to protect me. I wonder how differently he would treat me if he knew my full story and how many shapes I could turn into, including a dragon. "Then I'll just have to pretend I'm human."

He tosses his hands out to the side and enters the room farther. "But they don't like humans either. They treat them almost as bad a shape-shifters."

I shrug. "I can't see any other way. I'll just have to risk it. I know you can't understand how important it is to me to find out what happened to my parents."

He places his hands on my upper arms, holding me at arm's length, staring into my eyes. "I do understand. Despite my parents being pains in the butt, I love having them around, so I understand your search for your family. I'm just worried about you. I finally get to meet you, and you're leaving again."

I hear rustling behind him. I peer over his shoulder only to find a package shoved in my face. I balk momentarily then take the bag.

"I've packed some food for you to take."

I don't know when she managed to gather it, but I'm grateful. "Thank you."

"Simonne! What are you doing? That's rude." Andre places his hands on his hips and faces her.

I rest a hand on his shoulder. "No, it's okay. She's right. I should go and find the rest of my family, even the witch side."

He glares at his wife. "So, it was you who put this idea in her head."

She places her hands on her hips, her tone hard. "What of it? She needs to go. She's brought nothing but suspicion with her."

"She's only trying to find her family, trying to reach out and make connections with ones that should love her. Where's the harm in that?" He slams his fist on the bench, and the plates rattle from the force.

I place a hand on his arm that hit the bench, settling it before he has another outburst. "Seriously. It's okay. I do need to explore both sides of my family."

He about-faces to look at me. "You're not listening! Witches kill our kind. You're only one shape-shifter against a coven of witches. It's a ludicrous idea—a death sentence."

CHAPTER ELEVEN

Despite sounding confident, I am slightly nervous. Even so, I walk away with my head high. I've fought demons as a dragon and worked with the angels, although I haven't encountered witches before. They may be a completely different type of foe. With my pack on my back, I make sure my shoulders remain broad as I walk toward the forest, leaving the little village.

A small bluebird flies in front of my face and around my head when I reach the trees.

I swipe at it playfully. "You need to leave, cousin. I could accidentally squash you." I hold out my hand and compare the sizes. I chuckle. "Even my small hand is bigger than you are right now."

The bluebird circles a few more times despite my warning, flying from branch to branch just above my head.

"You don't get hints very well, do you?"

Two more bluebirds join the other bluebird and flap around my head.

I gently swipe my hand at them. "Come on, guys. This isn't going to change my mind."

One of the bluebirds circles down to the ground and hides behind a tree. I hear a strange noise before Yvonne's head peeks around the corner of a large trunk. I can see the side of her from her neck to her arm. She's doing her best to hide her naked body. "Andre told me to tell you that you must stay. You can't go to the witches. It's too dangerous."

As I walk past the tree, she moves her head around to the other side of the trunk, struggling to keep herself hidden and follow my progress as best as she can.

"I'm not changing my mind, Yvonne. I have to do this. There's nothing back home waiting for me. I need to find people I can be around and learn about my family."

Yvonne scoots toward the nearest trunk. "But Andre said he loves having you here. You should stay. He's part of your family."

"It's nice to be loved by one of the bluebirds. It's a shame his parents and his wife don't agree. Only a few people I've met in this village remotely want me to stay. That doesn't give me much confidence that the rest of the village will be so welcoming. Perhaps the witches will be different."

She jumps behind the next trunk, and I catch sight of a streak of her nakedness before she hides again. "No!" she almost screams. "You're making a big mistake. The witches won't be any better. They will definitely be worse." She dives behind another tree trunk.

Shaking my head, I halt and grab the pack off my back. "Yvonne, I can't have you running around naked like that. I have something in my bag for you." I dig through it until my hand lands on the items. I clasp them in my fist and pull them out. I reach my hand behind the tree and hold the items toward her. "Here. Put these on. I designed these specially for shape-shifting from a thread I came across. They're made for me, but surely they'll fit you too."

Her bare arm reaches around the trunk. She takes the clothing from me and holds it out, eyeing it curiously.

"They will shape-shift with you. It doesn't cover much. Still, it's better than what you're wearing now."

She frowns, her face expressing her disbelief as she studies the plain beige fabric. "Really?"

"Just put them on, would you?"

Her bare knees and elbows sporadically appear on either side of the trunk as she tries to slip the under-wear on.

"Trust me. I've tested them. Shape-shift," I say.

She shifts into her bluebird form and flies to a branch.

"What are you doing up there? Come down and shape-shift back into a human."

She flies down and lands behind a tree.

I roll my eyes. "You don't need to shift behind the tree. You can do it out here in the open."

Despite my encouragement, she shifts behind the tree into her human form—elbows and other bits of flesh show from behind the trunk. She gasps. "What's it made of?" She investigates her form as she moves from behind the tree, wearing a pair of blue underwear. They fit perfectly. She's much the same size as me only taller. "They're beautiful, and they're blue." She looks at me. "Were they blue for you too?"

"No. They're brown."

"Brown!" she exclaims, sounding shocked.

"Yes. Brown like a wolf."

"So, you're telling me that they change color to match the animal you are." She snaps the top band of her underpants, testing their firmness.

"Yes. They're made from a special fabric. Isn't it a relief you don't have to be naked now? You can shape-shift as much as you want, and you will always have some form of clothing on."

She smiles broadly. "I love it! You could sell these to all the shape-shifters and make an absolute fortune."

I pause in shock over the simplicity of it. "I don't know why, but that never occurred to me. It may be my best way to earn money. I was once told by one of my guardians that I should learn how to make a living. So far, I haven't needed to. The farm had everything I needed."

Another bluebird flies down and transforms behind a trunk, and Henri's face appears. "Yvonne, Andre sent you here to convince her to stay." He looks uncomfortable, staring out from behind a tree, but I don't have any spare shape-shifting underwear to give him.

She glares at him. "I'm trying. We were just talking girl talk for a few minutes. Give me a break. It's nice to have a set of clothes that stick with me no matter how many times I change." Yvonne turns back to me. "Ava, it would be good if you could stay. You seem like just the kind of person the shape-shifters of this little town needs. Perhaps it will bring the town out of a rut and help change their ways." She holds out a hand, and I grasp it.

"If things don't work out with the witches, I'll be back, okay? It's nice to meet a female other than my mother or guardian mother for a change. I haven't had the opportunity to meet many females."

A sad smile crosses her face. "Please come back, then you could be my sister—my sister from another mother."

"I'd like that."

Henri lets lose an aggravated groan. "Yvonne, you're supposed to be convincing her to stay, not return."

Yvonne lifts her chin. "Returning is better than not coming back at all."

"True, but convincing Ava to stay away from danger is even better."

I conduct a calming motion with my hands. "Guys, guys. I'm going no matter what." Glaring at the last bluebird flying around, I raise my voice slightly. "I promise I'll be back if things don't work out well. I'll probably be back to say hi to the people who do appreciate me, but I have to do this, and no amount of convincing will stop me. Even if you did manage to stop me now, it wouldn't stop me later on, and I'll have to kill my curiosity."

The last bluebird flies behind a tree and changes, sticking his head around the edge of a trunk to look at me. Both of the males continue to look awkward.

"I'm sorry, but I don't have any male shifting underwear. I gave my last pair to Yvonne. You'll just have to remain behind that tree, thank you." I give him a sly look.

Andre ignores my snide comment. "Don't go, Ava. You won't be safe."

"You won't be able to stop me. Sorry, cousin." I thread my backpack over my shoulders and continue on my journey. He shifts then sits in the branches above me.

"Thanks for the clothes," Yvonne calls after me.

Henri stands behind a tree, staring in disbelief as Yvonne walks around freely. In his bluebird form, Andre flies around my head a few times and picks at my hair. I swear and swipe my hand at him, causing him to chirp with alarm. I have no intention of hurting him, but I'm sure a sizeable human hand aiming for him would be scary at his size.

"As I said, there's nothing you can do, cousin. I have to investigate this part of my history. Perhaps Simonne will talk to you when I leave."

The bluebird circles my head and hovers in front of

my face for a few seconds, and I swear that I can see his sadness before he flies off again.

I forcibly pursue my path, ignoring the three blue-birds that hover around me. I push aside the concern for my safety and square my shoulders. It's challenging to continue to my unknown destination when I know these three will miss me. I'm not even sure of my reception into the coven. It sounds like almost a guarantee that it will be negative and unwelcoming.

CHAPTER TWELVE

I n the form of a bluebird, Andre flies in front of me.
He hovers as though trying to stop me when
another bluebird collides with him, knocking him out of
my way. The attacking bluebird shape-shifts into
Yvonne. "No, Andre! Sometimes a girl's gotta do what a
girl's gotta do. Let her go. She's a powerful shape-
shifter. Hopefully, she'll be okay."

I tilt my head at her in appreciation then continue
through the forest. I'm not sure of Yvonne's motivation,
but perhaps it's a good sign. Maybe she believes I need
to do this. After that, every bird that chirps sets me on
edge, making me think it might be another bird trying
to hinder me from leaving. It takes me a while to realize
that their attempt to thwart me is over. Andre has
finally given up the chase.

It's then that I realize how much I miss his interven-
tions. They were taking my mind off the witches and
how they may greet me. I know I'm a formidable oppo-

nent, yet I also know that I'm not familiar with the tactics of the witches, and I'm all alone. It's not as though I could ask Andre to come with me for protection.

A knot ties firmly in my stomach. I'm excited yet apprehensive. Perhaps the shape-shifters are wrong. Maybe more witches are like my mother. She must have siblings or relatives left in the coven.

When I'm confident that I'm alone and out of sight of the village, I pull my golden pin out of my hair. Strands of hair get caught, and I yank it roughly as I remove it from my head. I wince as the roots tear from my scalp. A bird screeches in a tree above. I jump. Surely, they can't be following me. I've been traveling for a good half a day and haven't heard, seen, or felt any eyes on me since I left the last little bluebird. It must be safe to pull out my broomstick.

I run my thumb over the leaves, observing the golden leaf hairpin in my palm, marveling over the details Zacharias embedded into the leaves. I unfold the pin to lie straight from the leaves and brush it with my witch's touch. It expands and changes into a golden-brown color with the leaves extending and forming into the spindly parts of the broom head. The part with the pin grows into the straight broomstick. I try to be modest as I look at it and marvel at the great invention I managed to make. It's spectacular how the tiny thing can transform. Clasping it in my right hand, I hold it out to the side in a horizontal position.

Clapping reaches my ears, and I frown as my heart

beats rapidly. This is not good. No one is supposed to see me do magic.

The clapping is slow and repetitive. "Bravo. Bravo."

Panic almost seizes me before I finally lay eyes on the sky-blue-gowned Archangel Gabriel.

"Oh, sweetie. That was a spectacular trick." Their crystal eyes adore me proudly. "Where on earth did you learn to do such magic?"

I place a hand over my heart. "Gabriel. You startled me."

The archangel tilts a hand at me. "Sorry, sweetie. I didn't mean to startle you. I merely had a feeling that you were stressed. I wanted to make sure you're okay. Excitement overcame me when I arrived in time to see you pull that trick. Is that a spell you made up?"

I nod. "It's something I concocted myself, but the rare secret ingredient is Zacharias's breastplate. He crafted it for me." I transform the broomstick back into the golden hairpin, leaving it on the palm of my hand, and hold it out to my visitor.

The archangel pinches it between their finger and thumb. "It's beautiful."

"Zacharias made the charm for me. He wanted me to wear it around my neck as something that I could call him with when in need." A deep sadness fills me, and I expel a deep sigh. "I changed it into a hairpin instead of a calling necklace. After all, these days, it's not like he'll turn up if I call him. He's earthbound and unable to travel far." My shoulders slump. "And he's changed."

Gabriel's crystal-clear eyes cloud over for a moment.

"Unfortunately, he's wallowing in self-pity. We hope he will pull out of it. What he's suffered is awful, but he's still capable of so much, even in his current state."

"Yes, I agree, but I don't know what's going to make him change. He won't even see me, which means if I call him through this charm, he definitely won't come."

"That may be true, for the moment. On the other hand, I find this fascinating. You have so many talents that I haven't seen in any other being before."

I raise an eyebrow at them. "Have you ever met a witch before?"

The archangel shakes their head. "Only you. And you're not a full-blooded witch, like you would have been if you were raised in a coven. So, I'm just as interested in what your outcome will be. Except my real reason is to be here as backup if you need me."

"Thanks, Gabriel. Although it's not like you can waltz up to the camp wearing those clothes with those massive wings on your back." I stroke the pale-blue feathers over the arch of a wing. "They are beautiful, but I don't think the witches will appreciate them, as we do." I slide the pin back into my hair. "You can walk with me for a bit if you like."

"I'd love to, sweetie." They fall into place next to my footsteps. "You know I wouldn't mind coming in with you."

"I know. However, I don't think it's a good idea. From what I've heard, the witches don't like anyone different from them. They might attack you and damage your majestic wings."

"I could throw a few shuriken at them." A surprisingly evil smirk marks the face of the archangel. "A few flying stars would put them off."

"Yes, it would put them off. I still don't want to risk it. We don't know what they're capable of, and maybe they'll throw them straight back at you. I don't know if you could deflect all of the shuriken at once, mixed with other weapons."

The archangel's face drops with shock. "Oooh. That sounds nasty."

A wry smile creeps on my face. "It's exactly what I used to do to Zacharias when he used to train me. I went through all the weapons within the vicinity at once. He would have trouble dodging all of them. There would often be a few that would sneak through his barriers because he couldn't spread it wide enough. I can curve the direction of the weapons."

With my thoughts returning to the seriousness at hand, I gaze at Archangel Gabriel in earnest. "I don't think I could protect you and me at the same time if that happened—although I would love your company. You always make interesting conversation."

As we walk, I gaze down at the archangel's shoes then at my own. There isn't much difference in the creativity of them. Both are flat and made with leather and a moccasin appeal. "I haven't noticed your shoes before. Do you always wear them?"

"No. They're crafted especially for this trip. It's my first step toward fitting in. I know I have a long way to go. In the meantime, I can still teach you how to throw shuriken. Even though you have many magical powers, it never hurts to have a little practical skill in case your spiritual powers die out one day."

Archangel Gabriel pulls the shuriken out of their never-ending enchanted pocket and passes me some. In slow motion, the archangel throws them and hits the different targets in the trees while explaining the processes as they do. I take a flying star and fling it as hard as I can. It slams straight into a tree trunk.

My companion nods. "Not bad for a beginner, but you need finesse."

I fling some more and use my magic to straighten their paths.

Archangel Gabriel raises an eyebrow when I face them. "You need to practice without using your magic, sweetie."

I grin. "I know. I was testing if you'd notice."

"Aha." They nod slowly.

After shrugging, I fling some more stars at the imaginary targets, each one hitting their mark.

"Good job!" Archangel Gabriel clasps their hands together, their crystal-blue eyes gleaming. "I had my doubts, but you've shoved them aside. You're a natural at flicking your wrist and throwing stars. Because you're so good at it, I'm going to give you some to take with you." They dive a hand into their pocket and pull out a handful of the shuriken, shoving them in my direction.

Tentatively, I open my hands and let the stars fall

into them. "Thank you. Are these stars made from anything of yours?"

Archangel Gabriel chuckles. "I'd love to say they were made from my breastplate, too, but as you can see, I'm not wearing one." They throw a hand over their mouth. "Oh. That's right. That's probably where it went —into these little stars. I've had them for so long, I'd forgotten about the breastplate I used to have."

I gaze at the archangel's unprotected chest and frown. "Don't you need a breastplate for the battles?"

The archangel tilts a dainty hand in my direction. "Oh, sweetie. Don't be ridiculous. I'm an artist, not a warrior. I don't wear stupid things like breastplates. That would wreck this beautiful gown. Anyway, I prefer to let others do the fighting. I just keep these stars with me in case the situation gets desperate."

"But wouldn't you need a breastplate in battle, just in case?"

"I don't get close enough to the blood and guts, darling. It's not in my nature. I prefer to throw these from a distance."

"Perhaps you should invest in a breastplate anyway, something dainty. I would hate for you to be hit in the chest. If something happened to you, we would certainly miss your bright personality."

"Aren't you sweet?" They stroke the side of my face affectionately. "Don't worry, sweetie. Nothing will happen to me."

Giving up the argument, I hold up the handful of shuriken. "I appreciate these. Thank you."

"Don't forget, if you need me, you can just call out to me. I attached a sensing charm to you. So, if you call out my name, I should be able to pick it up." The archangel's eyes are earnest as they stare deep into mine. "You don't have to face this alone."

CHAPTER THIRTEEN

After I convince Archangel Gabriel that I'll be fine, they dissipate, leaving me standing alone in the forest. Crickets chirp, eerily filling the silence as though alerting me of what's to come.

I pack the shuriken away in my skirt pocket and retrieve my broomstick. It's at least a good day's ride to the coven, and I'm surprised that my parents managed to meet. They lived so far away from each other. It must've been a chance meeting.

Half a day passes before I stumble across a small cottage. It looks exactly how Andre described it to me, and from my calculations, it's about the right location as well. It's literally in the middle of the forest, just like the cottage Zacharias built for me after the deaths of Piers and Caitline. Nothing but trees surround the area, making it the perfect hiding place.

It takes a moment to gather my courage to climb off my broomstick. The place looks desolate, as though it's been untended for approximately twenty years. No one must have lived here after my parents. Returning my broomstick to a bobby pin, I tuck it in my hair and circle the cabin, searching for a front door. It hasn't fared so well without regular maintenance, succumbing to the weather and possibly damage from when the murderers were here. Stones have crumbled from the sides, creating holes above the broken windows. The frames around the windows barely hang on to the stone walls. Gray slates lie crumbled on the ground, hiding in the long grass under a hole in the roof. The place needs some love and care.

Eventually, I stumble across an opening. The door barely hangs on its hinge and sits slightly ajar. I do my best to push it in farther and tentatively step through.

It's hard to believe that this used to be my home. Although, as I step inside, I spot the kitchen. Its cupboards are open, many of their doors hanging from their hinges, and the wooden benches have been worn down by the weather. A black pot oven sits deserted, void of life for some time. A quick flash of memory enters my head of times when this kitchen was whole in the years of my childhood.

I halt in the doorway. I'm keen to relive my childhood but tentative over what I might find. I never asked if someone came back to bury my parents. I hope so. After the reception I received from some of the shapeshifters, I can't be sure. Andre would've been too young to handle such a responsibility.

After taking a few deep breaths and smelling the

mustiness of the air, I press forward. There's only one way to do this—with courage. It's not like I am reliving their deaths, as I did with Jehan—although it almost feels like it. With each step, I turn my head to survey the rest of the little cottage. There's only one bedroom with an addition added in the half attic. That must have been my bedroom. I can see the broken stairs flowing down from the upper level.

Slowly I approach the main bedroom, the wooden floorboards creaking with every step. The door is only open a crack. It takes all of my courage to rest my hand on the door. Taking a deep breath, I ready myself for whatever I might find. A loud squawk screeches outside. I jump, holding a hand over my heart, and stare out the window. I must be more on edge than I thought.

Large black wings flutter as a crow takes off from a tree nearby and disappears into the forest. It almost feels as though it was watching me. I'm on edge, so it wouldn't surprise me if it's only my imagination running overtime. After my beating heart calms, I enter the room, the door groaning on its hinges and my nerves firing.

Dusty, moth-eaten bedspreads drape over the mattress in the bedroom. Squinting, I take a closer look. It appears more like a makeshift mattress, although it could be because of the gradual deterioration of the bed. Besides this, it seems to be the room least exposed to the elements. The rooms are absent of remains, filling my heart with hope that someone buried them. The hairs on the back of my neck prickle, and I gaze out the small window past the lace curtains hanging in shreds. The feeling of being watched remains. I'm not going to let it deter me.

Exiting the room, I reach for the ladder that leads to the room above. I climb a few steps until a rung crumbles under my hand, and my foot to drops to the rung below. My foot crashes through the step and onto the next, breaking that rung as well. I drop the broken piece as each rung underneath me rips from the sides, clattering to the floor with me. Not willing to risk a larger fall, I set up my broom and make it levitate while I stand on top, lifting me up into the room.

My head levels with the attic, and memories of my childhood flood back to me. The room is relatively dark except for a few small holes in the ceiling, but this doesn't stop me from seeing an image of me giggling with my parents inside this room as they read me a good night story. A warm feeling floods through my body, and I smile, welcoming the intrusion.

As the childhood memories flood back into my head, my eyes scan the room. The disappointment is sour when I see everything has been upended and disheveled. It's as though someone was searching for something. Probably me, if what the shape-shifters say is true. They wanted me dead as well, which would be a perfect explanation for the room's condition. They would've been looking for me.

I step onto the beams, being mindful of where I place my feet. Signs of rot taint each floor piece and, mixed with the stuff scattered on the floor, leave minimal walking space. It's only a few moments after taking in the condition of the room that a strong urge overtakes me. Suddenly, I don't want to be here. Quickly, I call to my broom, hook my leg over the top, descend into the living room, and exit the house.

A black form rises from the top of a fence and squawks as I storm past, chased off its perch by my appearance. It's the crow again. Maybe I wasn't imagining that I was being watched. I land the broom as it reaches the forest and watch it with narrowed eyes. Honing in on it, I see if I can pick up anything. I don't want any nasty surprises. The crow migrates farther into the forest, and when it doesn't reappear after a few minutes, I decide it must've gone.

I slide my converted broomstick back into my hair and walk the farmland. The fences are dislodged with rot, falling apart after years of standing untended in the weather. Long grass fills the paddocks, showing no evidence of animals for many years. It's unkempt and uncared for.

Weaving through the long grass, I walk between what look like they used to be paddocks on either side. I hear the cry of the crow in the distance and search for it. I don't see it with my human eyes, but I wouldn't be surprised if it sees me with its bird eyes. Crows have powerful vision. The temptation to change into a shape-shifting form and hunt it down is strong. I hold off. I don't know if it's a shape-shifter or something else.

Perhaps other witches out there can shape-shift just like me, but they're not well-known.

On edge, I continue around the yard and find two gravestones. My heart catches in my chest when I approach them, reading the names of my parents. I breathe a sigh of relief. At least someone had the decency to bury them. I kneel in front of them, mourning with long-overdue grief. There are no tears this day. I've lost so many loved ones in my life, and it all started here. With a shattered heart, I let my eyes drift to the side and spot flowers growing not far from the gravestones. I climb to my feet and saunter over, plucking them one by one before arranging them neatly and placing them in front of the tombstones.

"I love you, Mom and Pop." My voice breaks with emotion, and I close my eyes, giving them a rest from the painful sight.

"Are those your parents?" The voice is very close.

I jump, spinning around and searching for the surprise visitor. There shouldn't be anyone here.

CHAPTER FOURTEEN

An elderly man dressed in a long black garment flowing to the ground confronts me. A rope draws his garment around the waist, and his sleeves droop to his wrists. His matted pepper hair falls to his shoulders, and a tie in the middle of his long beard gathers the strands that fall to his chest. Dark-gray eyes peer from under drooping eyelids in a wrinkled and weather-worn face.

My mouth drops. "Who are you?" I can't stop staring at the sorrowful sight of him. A puff of breeze pushes from behind him, blowing his scent my way, and I screw up my nose in disgust. He may not have bathed in years.

His bushy eyebrow lifts as though he's intrigued by my question. "Which is what I was just about to ask you, young lady." His voice is husky, as though it hasn't been used for a long time, and his head jerks to the side slightly a couple of times. "But I see that I've surprised you, so I'll give you my name first. I am Yves." His eyebrow drops, almost sad. "But I doubt that would be of much significance at this stage." He indicates the tombstones where I laid the flowers only moments before. "And I asked if these are your parents." His head jerks to the side a couple more times, and I start to think this is an involuntary tic.

My nerves are firing again. I'm not ready to give away much about myself. Keeping my mouth shut, I stand poised, ready to either shape-shift or use a witch curse. I'm not sure how this encounter will go. Even so, I work hard to keep my wariness in check. If I show my distrust, it may make this strange man more defensive or aggressive. For the moment, I choose to remain human.

I study the flowers freshly laid on the two tombstones, and I reread the names on them before nodding. "Yes." I choke on the emotion.

A strange sentiment fills his dark-gray eyes. "I haven't seen you around here."

I shake my head. "No. I've been living elsewhere for quite a while."

"Since the day your parents were murdered," he says.

I can't hide my surprise as I glance at him. "How do you know?"

His head jerks to the side a couple more times. "I've been hovering around for years. I've kept an eye on the farm and the cottage ever since the day they died. I'm the one who buried them in this spot and engraved their names on the tombstones."

Subconsciously, I retreat from him.

A pained expression crosses his face, but he doesn't follow me. "I didn't see you here that day. I can't believe their family just left them in the cottage. Not one person came to bury them. They left them lying there, dead and bloodied." A deep sadness resonates on his face. "If I didn't live in the area, I would never have known, and I believe they would still be there to this day."

An involuntary shudder runs down my spine. It's a horrible thought that not one of my relatives cared enough to bury my parents. "Thank you for doing that, but what were you doing around this area?" Despite his claim that he did a good deed, I can't help but be suspicious of him.

"I'm an outcast." He eyes me from head to toe, and his head tilts slightly. "Probably much like you."

I back away farther. "What do you mean?" Before I can help myself, I ask, "Are you a witch? Although you can't be a witch because you're a male. Perhaps you're a shape-shifter?"

He ignores my questions and continues, "It was rumored that your parents were a shape-shifter and a witch married to each other and that this was their demise." His head tics again.

Annoyed that he dodged my question, I snap, "That doesn't concern you?"

His eyes don't stop scanning me, as though looking

for answers. "It would make me believe that perhaps, if you're their child, you're a mixture of both."

I flail my arms. "Have you ever thought that perhaps I am neither? Perhaps I'm just a human, and that's why the murderers left me alone."

He shakes his head. "No. Both sides hate humans just as much as the combined breed. You wouldn't be alive today even if you were human." His curious gaze doesn't stop. "No. I believe you would be part and part."

I place my hands on my hips. For a weird-looking guy, he seems perceptive. "What makes you think that someone who is half and half would exist?"

He chuckles, escalating my annoyance. "Why do you think I'm an outcast? I live in the shadows, hiding from all sides."

My eyes widen. "You're part shape-shifter and part witch?" I frown. "But you're a male."

His head twitches again. "No, not a witch, a wizard. A male version of a witch."

"Oh!" I exclaim. "I didn't know male witches existed."

He chuckles. "Females aren't the only ones with the gift—although there don't seem to be as many wizards as witches. How did you think witches are born?"

My cheeks warm. "To be honest, I hadn't thought about it."

"Why? You look to be of an age for breeding. Are you trying to tell me you haven't had this opportunity yet? Is that why your cheeks have turned bright red?" He smirks.

I frown. Who is this guy to be asking me questions like this? "No. I married. He's no longer with me."

"What happened?"

"He was murdered."

"By witch haters or shape-shifter haters or because of you?" A deep sadness seems to fill his wrinkled face again, and my distrust softens a little.

"I guess you can say it was because of me, not because of the shape-shifters and witches. It's because of other reasons. It doesn't matter why. It still breaks my heart."

"Of course. I'm sorry to hear that." His eyebrow lifts again. "So, do you want to tell me what you are?"

"Not particularly."

"Then why are you here all of a sudden?" His head tics to the side again.

"I'm trying to find out a little more about my parents. I have been to the shape-shifter side of my family but was mostly unwelcome and unable to find any answers. Now I'm heading for the witch's side. I've been warned against going there, although I still feel like I must."

He sits down on a large rock nearby. "Do you know where the witches are?"

Some of the tension falls off my shoulders. He may be strange, but he seems to be genuine. "I've got a rough idea, but I'm not completely sure. Do you know where they are?"

He points across the field. "They're approximately another day's travel, flying by broomstick, in that direction. You should stay. Let me make you a meal. Rest here for the night."

Even though my stomach rumbles at the mention of food, I gaze at him strangely, watching as another bout of twitches shakes his head.

He gathers wood from a nearby pile and heads toward a charred spot on the ground to stack twigs and logs on top of each other in the middle of the charred place. He rubs his hands together then gazes up at me. "Get ready. This tends to backfire."

A spark bursts from his hands, and he thrusts them at the pile of wood. The spark shoots from his palms, hitting the lower level of the collection. Dirt and shattered sticks explode from the ground, shooting through the air and covering us in fragments and dust.

I spit the dirt out of my mouth and gaze at him, dumbfounded. "What was that?"

He waves a dismissive hand. "Pfft. That was my magic. Impressive, isn't it?"

"Ah… yeah. I guess that's one way to look at it."

In a quick motion, he rubs his hands together again and thrusts his palms at the remaining stack. Dirt and fragments of wood repeat the process of exploding all over us. Dirt and twigs fall from my hair when I waggle my head.

He clasps his hands together again, and I yell, "No! Allow me."

An amused look crosses his face. "Is something wrong?"

I huff. "Let's just say you have an interesting gift." I restack the pile of wood, gather a tinder nest, and set to work rubbing a spindle onto a dry log. I'm determined to make the fire the human way, not ready to admit that I'm half witch. The friction takes time to spark, and when it does, I waste no time setting the stack of wood alight, exhausted by the effort.

"That would have been a lot easier if you'd used your magic."

"I don't know what you're talking about."

"Aha." He shakes his head. "Come. I will make you something. This is my favorite spot to cook. I don't particularly like entering the cottage, so I cook all my meals out here and sleep in the open."

Despite Yves's strangeness, my stomach protests when I think of leaving and only eating travel food. Yves ducks to the side of the barn and yanks something up from the ground, returning with a pot in one hand and a rabbit in the other. He lifts the rabbit. "I caught this earlier. I figured you would be hungry. I know I certainly am."

I hold my breath, my mind telling me I should leave and my stomach telling me I should stay. "I'll skin it," I volunteer, my head losing the battle.

He pulls a dagger from the back of his belt and hands it to me, hilt first, his head twitching. I go to grab it, and he holds it firmly, causing me to gaze at him to see why he won't let go.

"You can relax, you know. I'm not going to hurt you." His head jerks again. "I know I can come across as a little strange, but that's as far as it goes."

Not knowing what else to do, I nod. It's not as though I'm going to tell him he's giving me the creeps. He releases the knife, and I skin the rabbit on a nearby flat rock. I clamp my teeth on my tongue and hold my breath. Jehan and Zacharias spoiled me in the past— they would do this for me. As much as I enjoy meat, I hate killing or desecrating animals' bodies.

Yves disappears and returns with root vegetables and a flask of water. He takes the skinned rabbit from me and guts it, throwing it into the pot first. My stomach roars when the smell of cooking meat wafts toward me.

Yves stirs the pot with a long wooden spoon. "You should stay the night and travel again after a proper rest. You will need your wits about you."

I stare at his back, watching as his head jerks to the side. I wonder what caused him to have such a tic. "Thanks, but I want to get going as soon as possible."

He tilts his chin down and studies me as though looking over the rim of imaginary glasses. "What's the hurry?"

"I'm keen to find out who my real family is."

"You haven't known this long. I'm sure it can wait a night." His eyes don't leave me for a while longer. When I don't answer, he shrugs. "It makes no difference to me. I just know those witches are tricky, and it's best to approach them while you're alert."

"I understand. I can't say I'm looking forward to meeting them if things go wrong. I guess it's why I'm keen to get this over with and done."

He nods, his head shaking slightly in a strange direction. "Yes. That I understand. I've sampled their persecution before." He stirs the pot then adds the vegetables.

"You have?"

He doesn't look at me but nods. "Yes. It's why I have this twitch. I managed to escape their hold and ended up here."

I stare at him in silence.

"It's another reason I prefer to live in solitude, hanging out in a forest, hovering over an abandoned farm."

My heart swells with compassion. I was too quick to mark him off as strange. I should have thought more about how he ended up this way. "I'm sorry to hear that."

We sit in silence, both staring into the fire. After a while, Yves hands me a bowl of stew. I suck in the aroma. It smells delicious. Not waiting for a second longer, I scoop up a spoonful and blow on the hot food. After several mouthfuls, I ask, "How did you escape?"

He shrugs. "Just lucky, I guess." He pushes his spoon around in his stew. "I never want to go back there." His head twitches again. "They're horrible, horrible beyond belief."

I place my empty bowl on the ground beside the

stone I'm using as a seat. "Thank you for the stew. It was delicious."

He gazes at me from the corner of his eye then glances at my empty bowl. "You can stay. You'll be safe here."

"Thank you. I should go. There's nothing for me to see here other than ruins." I push off the rock and ready to leave but balk and turn back. "Since you've been hanging around here and were the one to bury my parents, do you know who killed them?" Deep down, I know it's a long shot, but I have to try.

The deep sadness returns to his eyes, and he shakes his head. "No. It happened on a day that I wasn't hanging around. I would come to visit this area quite often because I felt a bond with your parents. Often, I would watch them from the shadows, but on that day, I didn't. I left the farm to hunt. I would never pinch their animals, as healthy as they were." An uncontrollable tic overtakes him.

"Oh." Shivers run up my spine. I can't help thinking how odd that sounds for him to watch them without them knowing. Looping my bag over my shoulders, I head toward the forest.

He calls, "You can unpack your broom if you like. You'll get there a lot quicker."

Rotating rapidly, I gape at him. That's kind of creepy.

A wide smile covers his face. "Yes. I've seen you use it. I know you have some witching blood in you, and I saw you staring at me, and I recognized your suspicion after I cawed as a crow. You could have saved a lot of energy and started the fire with your powers."

I expel a frustrated breath. "So, if you've known from the start, why didn't you say so?"

He shrugs, looking impish. "I was seeing how quickly you were willing to give up information about yourself. You have a cautiousness about you, and that's good. You'll need it if you're dealing with witches and shape-shifters. I don't know who killed your parents, but I wouldn't trust either side." He touches the side of his head as though grasping something out of his hair. "It's quite a neat little broom you have. I love the hairpin you've disguised it as. I wish I could do that with something as simple as a bobby pin. Is it special material or something?"

I pull the clip out of my hair and unfold the pin, wishing the pin to turn into my broomstick. It doesn't disappoint. "Yes. It's a special kind of metal. I enchanted it myself. You won't find this metal anywhere, so don't try looking." Straddling the broomstick, I fly into the forest.

CHAPTER FIFTEEN

Thoughts of Yves wash over me as I travel to the witch coven. He acted like a stalker, making me wonder if he had a reason behind it. It puzzles me why he would spend days if not years outside my parents' place, continuing to watch the farm after they died.

Then at finding out he was doing the same to me, my feeling of being watched seemed not unwarranted. It puts me on edge to think he was the crow and had been watching me for quite a while. I have to pay better attention to any animals from now on. I'm not the only shape-shifter around, and I can't assume that an animal is just that anymore. It's too dangerous to remain naive.

While deep in thought, I barely dodge a tree and aim my broomstick to a less clustered patch of trunks. It worries me if he genuinely is an outcast because he's a shape-shifter and a wizard. Then what hope would my life hold? Perhaps that will be my life, too, living on my own in some secluded spot, only going out on missions when the angels call me.

After thinking long and hard about that, I realize the angels are more like my family these days than anybody. Ever since Zacharias set foot in my house, I've felt more loved by them than by anyone else other than my parents, my adopted parents, and Jehan. Those few beings haven't cared if I am part shape-shifter and part witch. They don't even care if I'm part human or all human. They've cared for me unconditionally, and they appreciate my efforts in helping them.

Grief-filled tears threaten to come, and I squeeze my eyes shut. Now they're all dead, except Zacharias, whose incarceration renders him almost as bad as dead. I wish I could get Zacharias to let go of his self-pity and become himself again, with or without wings. I miss him. He's like a father to me, and it hurts me every day to have him ignore me and shut me out. A small part of me empathizes with him, but a large part of me wants to smack him out of it. When I've finished my travels, I will have to try and call on him again and see if I can force him to see me or trick him somehow. He carried me through so much, and I wish he would let me do the same for him. Angel or not, he has a heart, and that heart needs comforting.

Darkness closes in, and I make camp. With a protective barrier in place, I curl on my side and pull my shawl over my shoulders, but sleep won't come. The noises of the forest are loud, and I spend the night watching every animal I see, wondering if they, too, are shape-shifters stalking me. It feels like the whole forest has come to watch me sleep, from bats to owls, even birds that usually only surface during the day, and the fierce creatures of the night.

Every time I'm nearly asleep, an owl hoots in the distance, or a bat chirps in the trees, eyes fixed on me as it hangs limply from a branch upside down. Sleep proves difficult in the open forest, making me think I would probably have been better off if I'd stayed traveling. It would be ideal if I could turn into a dragon, except a dragon isn't a native animal, and I'm still not sure if I should reveal my shape-shifter status. But if they're watching me, then that should make them shape-shifters as well. From what Yves said, near the witches' coven is the most dangerous and unlikely spot for shape-shifters. Perhaps it's just my mind playing tricks on me after what I've encountered so far. Eventually, I fall into a restless sleep and wake at the first hint of light.

When the sun finally peeks over the edge of the horizon, I'm glad to pack up my bed, have some breakfast, and be on my way. It's best to get this over with.

Flying toward the village, I catch a hint of smoke, and the trees eventually thin as I near the coven.

The nerves tear at my stomach. I don't know why I'm so anxious when I can do so many things as a witch and a shape-shifter. Maybe it's because I've never met a whole coven of witches before, and I don't exactly know what they're capable of. My witching ability is untrained and limited compared to a group that's trained together their whole lives, combining their knowledge and bettering themselves in their craft. What I have learned has been self-taught. I don't know if I possess excellent skills or bad skills in comparison to the other witches. My guardians and Zacharias didn't know anything about witches other than that they existed and they could be dangerous.

Dismounting my broom, I follow the smell of the smoke until it thickens.

Clattering pans accompanied by voices and cackles greet me. If it's the coven, they aren't hiding their noise and sneaking around. The closer I get, the stronger the laughter hits my ears, to the point that I want to cover them.

Reaching the edge of the forest, I stand among the trees, peering down into the small valley. There are several makeshift cabins in a little circle and a large firepit in the center with cauldrons sitting on the top, bubbling and boiling. Several women in long-sleeved gowns that fall to their ankles travel back and forth to the fire. I see a mixture of ages, mostly old and middle-aged. Eventually, I see a couple of young women, probably in their late teens. It's hard to tell their exact ages. I've heard that witches can often live for a very long time. Except for the women who aren't fully grown, the rest could be any age.

I'm mesmerized for quite some time, taking in all the different tasks they're undertaking. The place is bustling with activity, especially around the fireplace and over the cauldrons.

A twig cracks behind me, and I pivot. Something slams over my head before I can quench my curiosity, blocking my sight. I struggle and squirm in protest but am unable to free myself. I'm apprehensive about changing into a different shape and disappearing out of the bag in case the witches have captured me. The last thing I need to do is confess to being a shape-shifter.

"What do we have here?" The female's voice is high-pitched and rough.

"We have ourselves a little spy. Spying on the coven, are we?" asks another woman, her voice only slightly smoother than the first.

I struggle some more under the sack. "If you let me out of this, then perhaps we could discuss what I was doing."

What I said must be funny to them because they both cackle, hurting my ears. They yank me forward and drag me down the hill, proving they must be part of the coven. I allow them to drag me, stubbing my toe on different stones as we go. Each injury seems to make them laugh, proving my well-being isn't part of their concern.

The slope eases, and abruptly we halt. Rough hands grab my wrists, securing my arms behind me as they rip the sack off my head. I blink, trying to adjust my sight to the bright rays of light. It's hard to see exactly where I am.

"Look what we have here." The woman with the high-pitched, husky voice screeches, licking her lips lavishly. Her face is plain and young. Only the wisdom in her eyes betrays her age.

"What is it?" Another one asks, staring at me.

Several witches circle me.

One of the witches reaches forward and plays with strands of my hair. "She has shape-shifter hair." She pulls at the pale golden strands.

I notice the witches have hair all shades of dark brown. Not one is light brown or blond. "No." I lift my chin, faking strength. "I have witch's hair."

A witch calls from the left, "If you have witch's hair, then how did you let us capture you?"

I nod. "Yes. Exactly. I let you capture me. I wanted to come here to meet you all. Being captured was my ploy to enter the coven."

A grumble echoes through them.

Another witch with a mole on her cheek stands in front of me. "And why would you want to meet us?"

I fix my eyes earnestly on her. "I believe that I have your blood within my veins—the blood of this coven."

A witch behind me calls, "Not possible. You have blond hair. No one in this coven has blond hair."

"Well, I do," I say. "So, in that case, you're wrong."

The witch on the right stands tall. "The gall of her to call us wrong." Her voice is spiteful. I glance at her and see that her face is worn and wrinkled. She is old, even in witch years, and I'm sure just as stubborn. She's so old that she may be a witch elder.

I must convince them I'm not a shape-shifter. My brain whirls with thoughts.

"Of whose blood are you?" the old witch asks. "No one of true witch blood would challenge a coven like this."

Toning down my cheekiness, I try to present myself as ignorant. It worked with some of the shape-shifters. "My apologies if I've come across as defiant. I grew up on my own and don't know the ways of the coven. I have witch blood, and I believe it's from this coven."

The old witch's eyes narrow, making the wrinkles around them crease deeply. "Then who is your mother?" She edges her way through the crowd of witches toward my side and doesn't hide her suspicion.

"Suzanne is my mother."

A large gasp fills the coven. The old witch twists her head and spits. "She married a shape-shifter. You have shape-shifter blood. That explains the hair."

A witch from the left yells, "Let's persecute her!" Her hands rub together with glee. Her dark-brown eyes glare at me from a younger face, possibly the age of my mother. It suddenly occurs to me that I don't remember what my birth mother looks like. Because of this, even if I were staring at one of my relatives, I wouldn't have a clue.

A cheer erupts through the crowd. Several witches grab my arms harshly from behind, and they shove me toward the fire.

Firmly planting my feet, I hope to stop the progression. "No. I'm of witch's blood. You won't persecute me," I command.

A witch in the middle cackles. "A cocky one, ain't

she? No matter. We shall persecute you anyway, for being of suspicious nature—unless you can prove you're a witch." She licks her lips with anticipation.

Without a second thought, I survey the camp and pinpoint every single weapon I can see. From within, I reach out just like I practiced with Zacharias and command the weapons to point their sharp ends toward the group. This puts me in the center of the attack, but so many witches surround me, involuntarily making a shield for me with their bodies.

Despite my situation, I smirk. "If you don't believe me, then perhaps you should turn around and have a look at your surroundings." My smile grows wider as each witch spins to face the weapon pointing her way. Several gasps fill the air.

CHAPTER SIXTEEN

Pride possesses me, and I pull my shoulders back. Suddenly, the weapons careen with their sharp edges pointing to the sky. They shoot into the clouds before spinning and falling to the ground outside the group of witches. My mouth drops open, then I swallow a lump in my throat. Someone overrode my power.

The old witch's mouth twitches. "So, you can do a few tricks with some witch powers. If you ever point weapons at me or my coven again, there will be hell to pay. I will obliterate you." By the threatening look in her brown eyes, I can tell she isn't exaggerating.

I wriggle my wrists within their constraints. "I apologize. I didn't want to threaten your coven. I was merely proving a point. I have witch blood, and seeing as you're holding me hostage, it was the first thing that came to my mind."

"Point taken, but there are other ways to prove that

you're a witch." She flicks a hand at me. "You can release her for now, but keep her under watch at all times. Being the daughter of Suzanne, she has a lot to prove." She glares at me. "This doesn't eliminate the fact that you have shape-shifting blood."

The restraint on my wrists loosens, and my arms flop to my sides. I rub my wrists and watch the old witch shuffle away, her legs stiff from age. The coven separates, moving back to the things they were doing before I arrived. Two witches stand by my sides, their scowls fixed on me.

I huff. "Are you serious? You're just going to stand there and watch me the whole time?"

The chubby one on my right nods. "If that's what the high priestess says, then that's what we do. Everyone who enters our coven is under suspicion until proven otherwise, especially one with blond hair and a shape-shifting father."

I call to the old witch, "I'm merely here to find my family. I've been brought up by humans, and now I'm alone. I want to see where I belong. Can't you help me with that, priestess?"

She halts and pivots slowly to face me. "The witch coven is stronger than any blood running through your veins. Before being accepted, you must prove that you're part of this coven. I don't care which one of these witches is your mother or grandmother. It has nothing to do with anything, just like your blond hair doesn't prove that you're a shape-shifter, although it casts you into a more suspicious light." A strange smirk crosses her wrinkly face, and a chill runs through my heart. "We should string you up now and persecute you. Then we would see if you change into one under pressure." She hisses, moving her face only inches away from my own. She's so close I can see the open pores on her nose. Her mouth has barely any teeth left, and her breath stinks, but I understand each word clearly.

To remove the distraction, I stare straight into her eyes. "So, seeing as only the witch coven matters, I'm guessing you aren't going to help me find out who killed my parents? Even if it was one of your coven."

She cackles, then glares at me. "If it were one of my coven, I would tell you straight. We don't hide from murder. We take pride in it. And if one of my witches were the murderer, then your parents thoroughly deserved it. I wouldn't hide the fact."

"Are you telling me it wasn't one of your coven?"

"No. One of my coven would have boasted of the feat. Your parents were an abomination. Your mother marrying your father wasn't natural. It's not accepted. Shape-shifters are nothing but lowlifes. Witches don't marry, and they certainly don't stoop so low as to take a shape-shifter for a partner."

Staring at the old witch, I contemplate my reason for being here. The witches have clearly stated that they didn't kill my parents, nor are they willing to take me in and let me prove my dedication to the coven. Now that I'm certain they didn't kill my parents, I'm not willing to prove myself to these witches anyway. I've lived my life alone and without any rules other than human guidance, and I don't care to come under their law. "If that's the case, then perhaps I should leave now. I think it's best that I leave if you don't care for me or my parents." I move to go.

"You're not going anywhere. You stay here. We don't release shape-shifters, nor do we release anybody suspected of being a shape-shifter or human. You must prove that you're one of us and not a shape-shifter as well." She shrugs. "Sure, you did a little trick with the weapons, but that's not enough to convince us to let you live. It's our job to get rid of the impure. We should just delete you from existence immediately and save ourselves the hassle. We don't care if you live or die."

"And I don't care for your rules." I turn to leave again and find myself secured on both sides by the witches.

I flick them off, freeing my hands, and move forward again only to be recaptured. I flick off the grasp but am halted again. I turn my attention from the two witches and look for an opportunity to escape. The coven has surrounded me, determined to block my path. I don't want to shape-shift here. I would prove them right. Even if I escaped, they would pursue me until they found me.

It was a mistake to come here. They're holding me prisoner, and I'm still none the wiser about who killed my parents. Even though many shape-shifters were less than welcoming, I would have a better chance of finding family and people who care for me there. It kills me to think that one of the shape-shifters murdered my parents.

I face the high priestess. "Let me go. I'm nothing to you. You don't need to hold me."

She lifts her chin. "No. We won't release you. If you don't stay willingly, then I'll command your persecution to start immediately. It's your choice."

CHAPTER SEVENTEEN

Struggling with defiance, I straighten my back. It's the wrong move. They drag me to the priestess as she holds a metal clasp attached to chains and circles it around my neck.

A conniving expression passes over her face. "This metal is specially designed to stop shape-shifters from shifting. It fixes them in their human form, and because they are unable to change into their animals, they can't escape."

I wriggle, trying to back away from the hoop without success. The witches have my hands in a vice grip.

The high priestess smirks. "Yes. Why don't you change? Change into whatever animal you can change into. There may be hope for you yet."

I can tell she's lying. I'm damned if I change into an animal, and I'm damned if I don't. I wriggle some more, implementing my feet to force myself back.

The high priestess taunts me more. "Go on. Why don't you change? You won't be able to change after I've secured this around your neck."

Again I thrash, trying to pull away from the hands that grasp me from behind, but they're too tight. I desperately want to get away from the witches, yet I know if I change, the witch holding the dagger close to my ribs will stab me. Even though I can't see it, I can feel its flat side rubbing against my torso.

I balk, glancing over my shoulder, searching for what to do next. A click followed by chains draping over my body calls my attention back to the hoop now secured around my neck. My line of sight follows the chains draping from my neck to a spike in the ground not far from the fire.

The witch with the dagger pulls away, letting it hang loosely by her side. Instantly, my strength warps, and I find myself trapped. Using my witch powers, I focus on the dagger, pull it out of the witch's hand, and aim it directly at the high priestess.

I raise my chin. "Unchain me, priestess. I'm not yours to chain and hold captive. I don't belong to you."

The old priestess looks at the dagger aiming straight for her face. With one quick flick, she knocks it to the side. Her witching power is strong, proving she's had more practice than me. The dagger clinks against a rock not far from the fire, and I stare at it longingly.

The priestess saunters in my direction. "If you threaten me again, it will be your demise. Any weapon you threaten me with, I will instantly turn against you."

The witches who once held my wrists drag me by the chains close to the fire. The sun sneaks out from behind a cloud, and its rays instantly make me sweat. It isn't a pleasant place to be kept. I have no shelter from the elements. Somehow, I must escape, or the weather will wear me down.

"I was only trying to escape because I don't deserve to be chained. As you saw, I used witch's powers against you, not any other power. I didn't shape-shift, and I'm not interested in becoming a shape-shifter. I only want answers about my parents."

The priestess's eyes narrow. "You're staying as you are. You must earn respect to be released."

Suddenly, someone grabs my wrists from behind and fastens manacles around them. Chains secure them to the same post as the restraint for my neck.

I pull against the chains, only to stir my frustration. The shackles are weakening my magic. Only fragments of my power remain. "I don't know what you expect from me. I'm an untrained witch. I'm here only because I need help finding my ancestors and wish for training in our craft." I attempt to shape-shift to see if the priestess is lying. After their treatment, I don't think it matters if I expose myself.

I focus on becoming a swallow, an animal small enough it cannot be secured by the cuffs. It's difficult to concentrate with the narrowed eyes staring at me. Unsuccessful, I close my eyes and take a deep breath, focusing on every detail of the tiny bird. The pit of my stomach churns with disappointment when I don't feel the dissipating sensation that comes with a shift. The hard metal of the cuffs continues to rub against my skin.

Attempting to push away the disappointment, I narrow my focus, closing my ears to any of their negative sounds. I try again, focusing on a rat, only to be riddled with disappointment. Even though I try several more times to change into different animals, I open my eyes to find I'm still in my human form. I can't shape-shift into any animal. I can't even change into my dragon. How I would love to turn into that form to teach these witches a thing or two.

THE SUN'S RAYS INTENSIFY AS THE DAY DRAGS ON. A stream of sweat pours off my forehead and down my face. Without a tree within range, there is no reprieve from the harsh rays. The heat drains my remaining energy, and I crumple to my knees. I no longer have the strength to stand. It's been hours since they put me here, and not one witch has offered me a cup of water. Anytime they come near, they use it as an opportunity to taunt me.

I reach out to a pot lying not far away and beckon to it. Painstakingly slowly, it moves my way as I struggle to keep it upright. By the time it gets to me, I'm exhausted. I used so much energy in my effort to send my power past my cuffs. A flood of relief overcomes me when I see the pot is full of fresh water. The effort was worth it. The witches probably left it there to test the level of my power and determine if I'm a real witch. I drain the pot of its contents, grateful for the cool liquid that quenches my thirst.

A witch walks past and throws a spell straight at my torso. I'm unable to move my hands fast enough to block it. Dropping to my knees, I clasp at my stomach, which screams with pain. The witch throws another curse at my back. It arches, my body confused as to how it can protect itself. Gritting my teeth, I stifle a cry. I don't want to show weakness to these witches. I must pull it together. There's no one else to protect me and defeat them. I'm sure the shape-shifters didn't follow me here. I wouldn't want them to. They would be risking their lives for me.

I straighten my back and crouch rigidly on my feet. Now that I've quenched my thirst, my mind sharpens, taking in the actions of the witches and making mental notes of any ideas to escape. It's tempting to use my gift of invisibility, but that would only raise questions. Even if I could maintain the spell, someone would eventually spot my neck restraint floating in the air. It may not be a good spell for them to learn if they don't know about it already, and I have no plans to teach them new spells.

I sit and continue watching, learning about the witches and what they're capable of. It's the only way I can outsmart them. It's clear they aren't going to treat me as a fellow witch.

I ignore the jeers as each witch passes, making sure I

remain alert to dodge any spells flying my way. Instead, I listen to any incantations and the actions they use to execute them.

Slowly the sun's heat loses its intensity as it disappears over the horizon, filling the sky with beautiful hues of orange and pink and blue as it says goodbye for the night. The beautiful sight relieves some of my distress. A chill travels through the night air, raising goose bumps on my skin. I long to rub my arms to warm them but am unable to do so.

The witches cook their meal over the fire before me then eat without sharing a morsel with me. They shower me with another set of insults before they retire to bed, leaving me with the calls of the nocturnal animals for company. An owl hoots in a tree lining the outside of the camp. A bat screeches in the branches farther in the distance, followed by the caw of a crow. I search the blackness of the sky. I didn't expect a crow to still be making noise. They usually sleep soundly at night, though it's possible it could have been disturbed by something.

The crow caws again, and it reminds me of Yves at my mom and pop's house. I push the thought away. He wouldn't be here. Not even Andre or the shape-shifters are here. It's only my imagination or wishful thinking. Nobody I've met recently cares about me enough to follow me into a witches' coven. Although, even though I don't know him well and think that he's a little strange, I would be thrilled to see him right now.

The crow caws again, and I gaze in that direction. I

can't see anything other than trees. Weariness over-comes me. I give the chains another go, trying to loosen them so I can lie down. They don't budge. I yank at the chains one last time without success. Defeated, I sit on my heels and stare into the forest as my eyelids droop.

CHAPTER EIGHTEEN

A noise startles me out of my pained sleep. I remain chained to the spot not far from the central fire. Without the scorching heat bearing down on my head, I can think a little clearer. A crow calls in the distance as my mind ticks over ways to get out of the situation. It works its way through all the circumstances and people I've met that led me to this position.

I remember the time the Archangel Gabriel visited me last and how they gave me some of their shuriken. I'm so used to using witch power and shape-shifting that I completely forgot about them. With my hands tied securely, I've been unable to reach anything on my body. That includes the spot that itches profusely at the back of my leg. Luckily, I have one advantage. I have enough of my witching powers available to draw the flying stars out of my pocket.

Exercising my skills, I reach down, searching every pocket in every section of my clothes until finally I find the pocket I placed them in. I draw the shuriken into one bundle and pull on the clumped metal items sitting deep in a hidden pocket in the folds of my skirt. It's a tricky process trying to weave them from the depths of the material without slicing the fabric. When I perfect the process, I let the flying stars drop to the bottom of my pocket again.

A witch of medium height comes out to the fireplace. She saunters close, her hips jerkily rocking from side to side. It's a strange, confident sort of walk. Her eyes are glued to me, tormenting me as they travel up and down my body as though sizing me up. From the look on her face, I expect her to do something sinister at any second.

I feel stronger and more confident than I did during the heat of the day. Tightening my back muscles, I sit straight and focus my magic on the rise and fall of the shuriken. Knowing they're there and accessible keeps me calm. I almost wish she would taunt me and give me a reason to send the bladed weapons her way.

I cock my head to one side, giving her a wry smile.

My taunting and daring seem to work. Either that or the witch had mean intentions anyway. She walks within a couple of feet and stops, whispering something under her breath. I brace myself. It reminds me of the process I used to make myself invisible when I was young.

A sudden surge hits me, sending the feeling of nails piercing my flesh deep into my skin. The sensation is real, causing me to search for blood and the source of the pain. Nothing other than clothes touch my skin. There are no holes, no nails. Nothing is physically boring into my skin, yet the pain is unbearable. A scream rises to my throat, but I force it down with sheer pride. I grit my teeth and will myself to focus on the shuriken, imbuing them with my power and lifting them out of my pocket in one clump. When they break free from the material of my gown, I send them flying straight into the witch.

I stare deep into her eyes, my teeth gritted with pain and my eyes shooting daggers of hatred. I watch as the shuriken embed deep into her skin, slicing through her face and arms, leaving large gashes. Blood pours from the cuts before I release the last few shuriken, which slice deeply into her torso. One shoots straight into her heart. In the witch's final few seconds, her face changes from a nasty snarl to openmouthed amazement as she stares at me before collapsing, her blood spilling onto the dirt.

It happened so quickly she couldn't cry out, although I'm sure the shuriken that passed through her voice box didn't help. Using my witch power, I call the shuriken back into my pocket and tuck them away. Resting my bottom on my heels, I observe my master-work, almost daring the next witch to torment me. If I have to, I will eliminate these witches one by one and somehow figure out a way to get out of these chains. Heaven help them if I get out of these chains before-hand. I will shape-shift into my dragon, then we'll see who's more powerful. In hindsight, I should have done that from the start. Out of stupidity, I was willing to give the witches the benefit of the doubt.

I wait, chomping at the bit for the next witch to approach. I'm tired of being tied up. I can see the shape-shifters weren't exaggerating when they said the witches are unfair in what they do to shape-shifters or outsiders. Whether they're related to my mother or not, I look forward to making them pay.

Even though darkness has fallen, I'm surprised over the lack of witches coming to the fire. I had thought they would practice magic around the fire before going to bed. Perhaps these witches keep such an unusual routine that they don't have regular timetables, or maybe they hate each other so much that they can't work together often.

I wait. The time passes slowly. The night air brings an intense chill, leaving me thankful for the heat of the fire. Still, the witches don't come.

Silence fills the camp, leaving only the crackling of the fire and the call of the wild animals. Eventually, the faint rumble of a snore rises from one of the closest cabins. It's the cabin I assume the old witch disappeared into. The moon is late rising, and there's no light in the sky.

I pull against my chains, trying to maneuver my hand into some unusual position that will allow it to slide through the hole. Try as I might, I can't compact my hand to the size of my wrist so I can pull it through. Frustration oozes from every pore. My shape-shifting powers are stuck while this chain is around my neck. I try to use my witch power to unlock it, but it doesn't budge. The hoop must require a witch's signature to unlock. Either that or a unique key.

My shoulders slump with discouragement until it suddenly dawns on me. Maybe I could call its key. I assume that the old witch has it in her cabin. I reach out with my mind, searching for the metal in the shape of a key. I assess everything that radiates metal within the area. With the power-dampening wrist cuffs on, it takes all my strength, but I manage to open the high priest-ess's cabin door and maneuver each metal item out, one by one. The first thing I remove is a mug, then a bowl, then some sort of spoon, even a knife. Nothing I remove turns out to be a key, and each item disappoints me more.

I try the next cabin, then the next, hoping to find it in one of those. Each one turns up as fruitless as the other. I'm concentrating so hard on finding the key that I am startled by a twig cracking behind me. I switch my power from searching to attacking as I aim it at the noise behind me. My witch's force is about to connect when, suddenly, I realize it isn't a witch behind me. At the last second, I pull it back.

"Phew. That was close," the man whispers, his face blanched against the night sky.

"Yves! What're you doing here?" Even though I don't know the man well, I'm so grateful to see him. He's the first pleasant face I've seen since my parents' cottage.

His head twitches, jerking to the side. "I couldn't

just leave you here to rot under the witches' care. I knew they wouldn't look after you." He glares at me from under a raised eyebrow. "I do believe I told you that."

"Yes. You did, but I was determined to see if I could find answers. Normally I'm not so defenseless."

"I figured as much, seeing you travel alone. You would have to be powerful or stupid to travel alone, and you don't appear to be stupid to me." His eyes dart around the camp, undoubtedly looking for any threats. His voice lowers farther. "But even the powerful can be brought down by a group. Nobody is invincible."

I smile and whisper, "I'm happy to see you, but you can't get caught too. I'll never forgive myself if they hurt you because of me. I've had enough of that in my life."

He waves away my comment. "I'm an old man who flies around a deserted house, spying on people that pass through. I have nothing to live for."

"Everyone has something to live for. Otherwise, we would all give up on our lives much earlier."

He huffs, looking unconvinced. "How come you haven't shape-shifted out of those chains?"

"This neck brace won't allow me to shape-shift. Somehow, it's holding me in this form. I'm stuck. I can't get it off. It won't react to my witch's power. There must be a key for it somewhere."

Yves walks up to me and studies the circle. He pulls on the chains welded to the ring around my neck, trying to loosen them, but they don't budge. He leans over me to get a better look and stiffens when a crackle spits from the fire and makes me jump. Frantic, I search the area. Nobody's around.

He chuckles softly. "We're a bit on edge, aren't we? We don't need noises like that right now." He focuses back on the chain, yanking and twisting it in different directions. "I could try my magic on it."

"No!" I say too enthusiastically and louder than I anticipated. Nervously, I study the witches' cottages before me, my heart beating rapidly. Thankfully, no one comes our way.

Yves stands back and smirks at me. "What? Don't you trust my magic?"

I hold up my palms. "No offense, but I saw what you were capable of back at my parents' place." I tug at the neck collar. "These are fastened a little close to my vital organs for me to be comfortable with you trying your magic on them."

He shrugs and pulls a little pin out of the rope tied around his waist and sets to work on the clasp.

I study his wrinkles of concentration in the firelight as I wait. "How's it going? Are you having any success?"

"Unfortunately, there's no keyhole. I don't know how it's joined, but it's firmly fixed. I'm trying this metal pin to see if I can push it apart, but it's not working." He pushes and pulls some more, the weight of it pushing against my throat.

He gasps. "Oh. I managed to get inside the slot. I'll keep wriggling to see if I can pry it apart." His voice remains a whisper to avoid any unwanted attention from the witches. The roughness of his hand rubs back and forth, bumping against my neck, grating along my skin with every movement.

Something snaps, and his hand jerks forward. "Drat! It just broke, and the end is stuck in the little slot."

My shoulders slump forward in defeat. "There has to be a way out of here."

He leans over me some more, intently studying the loop around my neck. He's so focused even when he twitches that my heart swells with admiration. Trying to help however I can, I keep a lookout for any witches and cross my fingers, hoping he will find a way to unlatch the clasp.

A crack sounds on the other side of the fire, and my body stiffens. I glance in that direction in horror. I curse. A witch stands on the other side of the fire. Somehow, I missed her. She flings her arm out toward Yves.

"Duck!" I fling my body at him to knock him aside.

His body slams to the ground, and he grunts and rolls to the side. He moves quickly for an older man.

Instantly, my mind shifts down to my pocket with the flying stars, and I fling them in the witch's direction. My aim is accurate, and her body falls not far from the first witch, the same look plastered on her face as she hits the ground.

This line of defense is sufficient when only one witch comes out at a time, but if several witches approach at once, I don't like the odds. Right as I'm thinking this, another strange noise sounds behind me, and my heart seizes in panic. Yves is behind me and, as far as I know, can't do anything to protect himself other than change into a crow. Against these witches, that isn't a defense. Hunkering down, I twist and search for the noise.

CHAPTER NINETEEN

A cluster of blue circulates a few meters away. From his crouched position, I sense Yves is going to shift.

I hold my hand out to him. "Stop, Yves! It's okay. This one is with me."

Yves's expression is tortured as he hesitantly stares at the blue figure.

"Archangel Gabriel, it's so good to see you."

Yves glances at me out of the corner of his eye. His survival instinct is screaming at him to leave, the torture of deciding what to believe clear on his face.

I smile at him only to have the gesture returned with a whispered, "Archangel?"

I nod. "Yes. Archangel Gabriel. One of my true friends."

The crackling of sticks and leaves grows closer as the archangel rushes toward me. "Oh, sweetie. How did you get into this mess?" Warm hands brush the skin of my neck as the archangel pulls at the clasp.

I tilt my head to the side, giving them a more unobstructed view. "This is my mother's side of the family. Clearly, an open welcome." Sarcasm drips from my voice.

Archangel Gabriel pulls at the cuff, and it chafes my skin. "How come you haven't shape-shifted and gotten out of this brace?"

"Somehow, this shackle dulls or restricts my shape-shifting abilities. It's specially designed so they can capture the shape-shifters and restrain them. Once they capture shape-shifters in this brace, the shape-shifters can't escape, and the witches can persecute them."

Archangel Gabriel's mouth drops open with disbelief, and I nod.

"Yves tried to undo the brace but hasn't succeeded."

Both of Archangel Gabriel's soft, dainty hands clasp the brace around my throat. They close their eyes and frown, deep in concentration.

Hissing reaches my ears over the crackling of the fire, and I glance over the flames. I gasp. Several witches approach, their arms poised and ready to strike.

"Oh no," I whisper, pulling my energy from its source and directing it at the shuriken.

Archangel Gabriel's hands drop the brace around my neck, and they huff. "These witches need to be taught a lesson." Strange malice edges their voice as they flick their dainty hands at the witches. Suddenly, the witches shoot into the sky, hovering several feet high without their brooms. They are quite some distance away, yet I'm sure horror is plastered on their faces as they hover helplessly in the air.

One of the witches circles her arms as though winding up a spell, and I pull on the shuriken with my magic, ready to retaliate.

"Nuh-uh-uh." Archangel Gabriel shakes a finger at them. "If you shoot any of us, then I will let you fall, and you won't have your brooms to catch you."

The witch's face turns pale and expressionless, too scared to show any other emotion, then she drops her arms limply at her sides.

"You may be witches," Archangel Gabriel says. "But you can't fly without your brooms." The archangel gazes around the cabins and seems satisfied when they find the campground empty. "Now, I can see you haven't given this young lady a warm welcome, so I'm taking her away with me."

"You will never be able to undo the brace!" the youngest witch yells down at us.

"Really?" Archangel Gabriel lifts a blond eyebrow. "Now, I'm not usually into torture. I don't like all that mess." They flick their hand dismissively. "I prefer a distant kind of fighting or no fighting at all. It messes with my creative brain." They gaze at their trimmed fingernails. "So, one of you had better speak up immediately and tell me how to undo this brace. Then we'll be on our way without any bloodshed on your part."

"Blood will be shed on your part, though." The high priestess's voice sounds from the corner of the camp. Her arms flick at us, sending some kind of spell. Archangel Gabriel immediately secures a barrier and sends a white pulse directly at the witch. She flies back several hundred feet into a tree, slamming up against the trunk's bark, and flops lifelessly to the ground. I don't know if she's dead or just stunned, but right now, I don't care.

Archangel Gabriel sighs. "There's always one in a crowd, isn't there?" They look up at the hovering witches. "Now, tell me. How do I take this off?"

"You've just ruined your only chance." The witch in the middle calls down. "She was the only one who could open it. She was overcautious in that way, you know, because witches trust nobody, not even their own kind."

Archangel Gabriel gazes at the old woman and sighs loudly. She remains limp and doesn't move. "I'll just have to find another way around it. Let me know if someone else approaches, okay, sweetie?"

I nod.

The archangel closes their eyes. Both hands wrap around either side of the neck brace and the joint. A glow escapes their hands then encases the metal, glowing brightly until finally a click sounds, and the weight drops from my shoulders.

"There. That should do it." Pride seeps through Archangel Gabriel's voice. Holding the cuff between their forefinger and thumb, they daintily droop it from their hand as though it's something offensive then fling it toward the fire.

It's nice to see it gone, even though the fire likely won't do anything to the metal.

Immediately I shift into dragon form and take to the sky, hovering only a few feet away from the witches still stuck in midair. I breathe a plume of fire in their direction as a warning, not quite far enough to touch them. They cringe from my heat, covering their eyes and face in shock and horror.

"You're a dragon!" gasps the witch who attempted to cast the spell at Archangel Gabriel earlier. She's not sure who to consider the biggest threat, me or Archangel Gabriel.

I breathe another plume of fire in their direction, warming the air just under their feet. They tuck their heels under their bottoms, flinching from the heat. I then swoop down and nudge Yves onto my back. Surprisingly, Archangel Gabriel jumps on my back behind Yves, and I take to the sky. I don't ponder why they choose to ride when they could have flown themselves.

Squeals of delight project through the night sky from Archangel Gabriel as we lift higher. Laughter rumbles through my giant belly, and I accidentally spit a column of fire when I open my mouth.

The archangel turns and releases their hold on the witches, lowering them to the ground. Facing forward, their eyes filled with delight, they pet my scales. "I've always wanted to ride a dragon."

I peer over my shoulder, spotting the witches in the

distance staring up at us, still stunned and plastered to one spot.

Archangel Gabriel follows my line of sight and calls to them, "Oh, don't bother trying to follow us. We'll kill you if you do!"

Knowing there's nothing for me here, I fly back the way I came, riddled with disappointment in the last stretch of my journey. Even if the witches had any information about my mother, they weren't willing to share it. Despite being warned, I didn't think that all witches would be so bad.

It's difficult, but I hold on to some hope that perhaps I just had a bad experience with witches. Maybe good witches in the group don't shine forth because they're afraid. I don't know, but I'm not going to get anywhere trying to hang around the camp, so I flap my enormous green wings back to where my parents lived.

The moon disappears behind a cloud, and my dragon sight kicks in, enabling me to see in the dark. I scan every bit of land as we fly back to my parents' home. Someone taps my back, and I turn my enormous head to gaze over my shoulder. Archangel Gabriel has a wide, brilliant smile plastered across their face.

"Hey, sweetie. Would you mind doing a dive? I could certainly use some thrills in my life."

I gaze quickly at Yves. His face is expressionless, his eyes wide. I'm not sure if he's happy or not. I nod then fly higher before collapsing my wings and nose-diving to the ground. Our speed builds as we near the surface.

Even for me, it's exhilarating. The adrenaline pumps through my body, lifting my spirits.

Archangel Gabriel calls out in excitement, lifting a hand as their legs wrap around my neck, and the other hand clasps the spikes on my back.

I glance over my shoulder and see Yves looking nervous. At least he can change into a crow if he falls and fly down to safety.

When I almost hit the ground, I open my wings, and we level out for a while before I tilt my nose up to the sky and flap my wings, raising us up high again. It feels so nice to be free again after being tied up so humiliatingly by the witches.

The distance to the cottage is chewed up quickly by my enormous wings, and spotting the farm in the distance, I aim my nose directly for the clearing next to the farmhouse.

As soon as we land, Yves and Archangel Gabriel climb off my back. I change into my human form, cloaked in my shape-shifting underwear.

Yves stands before me, his eyes wide. "You have a lot of explaining to do."

CHAPTER TWENTY

He yanks back the hood of his black gown, exposing his long gray hair, his legs spread wide and his hands on his hips. "All right. Tell me everything!" The bushy gray eyebrows push together. His eyes flick from Archangel Gabriel to my shape-shifting underwear and then back to me. "Not only do you keep company with angels"—he shakes his head —"which I've never seen before, but you're also a dragon. Have you heard how rare that is?"

Fixed to the spot, I remain silent, not knowing quite what to say. After a few moments, I shrug. "To be honest, I don't know anything about what I should or shouldn't be doing. I was raised by human parents. I knew nothing about dragons. The shape came to me accidentally after my twenty-first birthday." I raise an eyebrow at him. "Perhaps you should be the one explaining things."

He huffs, and his head twitches to the side. "You

can't get out of it that easy. What about that?" He points a finger at Archangel Gabriel. "What about the angel? I'm not sure if it's a male or female. Otherwise, I would say."

A broad smile spreads across Archangel Gabriel's face, and they move forward playfully. "Actually, I prefer to be called *they*. Male or female, it's all part of the perception." Archangel Gabriel's tone is pitched at the perfect level that leaves the listener undecided as to whether they are male or female. Their curly blond locks fall, framing their face and landing softly on their blue padded shoulders. A hint of amusement gleams in their eyes, which appears when people try to work out if they're male or female. Despite many questions, the archangel refuses to define themselves. "Does it matter if I'm male or female?" The archangel tilts their head to the side, questioning Yves with crystal-blue eyes.

Yves looks confused and a little set back. "No. I guess not. It's just easier to refer to you by male or female terms. Being an angel, I guess you can do what you want."

"I wouldn't say I can do what I want, but this is one way I define myself, and I have fun with it." The archangel looks at me. "Don't I, sweetie?"

I can't help but grin. I haven't had much to do with them, but the little I have, I knew the archangel to be lighthearted and have a sense of humor. I always appreciate their company. I nod.

Yves shakes his head, looking as though he's trying to clear it, then looks at me with confused eyes. "Anyway, I demand answers. Why are you associating with angels? And what else can you turn into or do?"

"My association with angels started when the angel leader, Archangel Michael, sent one to guard me when I was young. Zacharias lived with my family and watched over me growing up. He protected me after the murder of my guardian parents. He watched over me, basically raising me and acting like a father for quite some time. He guided me and protected me until I could shift into a dragon. He didn't know the real reason behind the mission, but the angels knew they must protect me."

"Yes, that's right." Archangel Gabriel moved slightly closer. "The angels get a lead, and they follow it even if they don't know the full meaning behind it."

Yves looks at Archangel Gabriel. "Really?"

The archangel nods. "It's true. Archangel Michael didn't send just any angel to protect Ava. He sent his right-hand warrior. Zacharias was the most powerful warrior under Archangel Michael, and he guarded her and held her under his wing"—they smirk at their pun —"so to speak, until she came of age and was able to protect herself.

"It was after this time that we stumbled across her power to turn into a dragon. It was discovered by accident as he was training her to fight and protect herself." Archangel Gabriel runs a hand gently down Ava's cheek and smiles. "It was by Ava's determination that she was pulled with Archangel Zacharias onto the battlefield of angels and demons fighting. From there, she became a very successful warrior, helping us defeat the demons overtaking the earth."

Yves remains silent, staring at me with his mouth open. He looks completely lost for words.

The androgynous angel gently lifts the man's chin, shutting his mouth, and continues, "Other than her late husband, you are the only human to know about her activities. She has fought in many battles, saving us from demons and endangerment or near-extinction. The day that she first encountered the battlefield, much to Archangel Zacharias's disapproval, the demons were so powerful that they could've wiped us out. This event was one of the main turning points. She's precious to the angels, and naturally, we continue to watch over her at certain stages. If she's ever threatened, like what just happened, of course, I'm going to come to her aid."

Yves's eyes are wide. "That's incredible. I've never heard anything like it before. I thought angels could fight their own battles."

The blond curls sway as Archangel Gabriel nods. "We can still be defeated. The right enemy can bring us down. When Ava stepped onto our fighting field, she brought a weapon the demons hadn't encountered before."

Yves turns to me. "Are you just a dragon as a shape-shifter, or do you have other shapes?"

I can't see any reason to distrust him at this stage. He followed me into the witches' coven and tried to rescue me. Even though he failed, the fact that he followed me and tried to help shows I can trust him to a point. After seeing me as a dragon, I don't think he would be stupid enough to try and deceive or betray me. "I can shape-shift into any form I want."

I didn't think his mouth could drop open any wider, but it did. "A dragon is an extremely rare shape-shifter, and to be able to shape-shift into multiple forms is just as rare. Those traits combined make you an extraordinary witch and shape-shifter. I wouldn't like to be up against you. That's for sure."

Archangel Gabriel chuckles. "That's an understatement." They hold their stomach, and their chuckling intensifies.

Yves glances at the archangel, his eyes sharp with disapproval. "I'm glad you find me funny."

"Oh no, sweetie. It's not you that I'm laughing at. I'm just laughing at the fact that no one would want to go up against her. The witches were just lucky that she half submitted because she was keeping her shape-shifting side a secret from them. If she had given up the facade, she would have scorched them on the spot. They were stupid to treat her like that. Now they've made themselves a worthy enemy. If she didn't have such a good heart, they would be in serious trouble." The archangel chuckles again. "If she had a witch's heart, as they expected, the coven would be seared to the bone by now."

"Oh. I can see your point," Yves says, his head twitch returning. "I am awed to be in your presence then." He half bows toward me.

I wave a hand at him. "Don't be ridiculous! I'm just

an ordinary person somehow endowed with these gifts."

"But you also associate with angels," he says.

"You heard Archangel Gabriel. It's only because they decided to associate with me."

"Yes, because you're special," Yves argues.

I roll my eyes. "Clearly, we're not going to get anywhere with this argument. You're wasting your time classing me as special. I'm merely a young lady searching for her family and answers to questions about her parents' past."

"Say what you want, oh special one." He tilts his head down, as though giving a mini-bow.

"Oh, don't be ridiculous!" I say. "Can we forget this nonsense and rest for the night? I'm a little tired after what we've been through."

"Oh, of course, Your Majesty." He bows, and his hood falls over his head, covering his gray hair. "I'll prepare you some dinner."

I roll my eyes before being distracted by a chuckle off to the side.

Archangel Gabriel grasps their stomach again. "I like this one. He's got a sense of humor."

Yves glowers at him. "I'm not being funny." He spins to face Archangel Gabriel directly.

"Maybe not, but it's still hilarious."

CHAPTER TWENTY-ONE

Mixed hues of the sunset paint the sky in deep golden orange, blue, and red. As though in unspoken agreement, we set up camp in the clear patch not far from the cottage and away from the overgrown paddocks.

Even though the cottage offers some shelter, I can't bear to sleep inside. Seeing the destruction is a reminder of my parents' murder, more loved ones ripped away.

After the distressful day yesterday, we spend the day recuperating by lounging around and sleeping. In the afternoon, I catch a few pheasants in my wolf form and bring them back as my contribution to the meal. Even in wolf form, it upsets me to kill animals, but I have to eat. Yves roasts the birds, and as we eat, Archangel Gabriel wanders around, observing the area and the empty pens overgrown with weeds and grass.

The dainty archangel motions to the pens. "Whatever happened to all the animals that were in these pens?"

I glance at Yves expectantly as I shovel a mouthful of food past my lips.

He throws his cleaned pheasant bones into the fire without looking up. "They were picked off by wild animals one by one, and in my crow form, I finished off their remains."

I choke on my mouthful and thump my chest, trying to dislodge the food and stop the spluttering.

Yves looks at me. "I couldn't let the meat go to waste. Besides, I was hungry."

I manage to stop my spluttering. I clear my throat and shake my head. "It's not that. It reminds me of my animals at my cottage. I set them up with food and water but didn't put up a ward to protect them. I hope they're okay. I know I eat animals for food, but I don't like them coming to harm, as ironic as that sounds." I toss a cleaned bone at the fire and watch the flames crackle when it disrupts the embers.

Yves nods, then his head twitches, making him look uncomfortable. "I understand. That's why I finished off the remains. It was perfectly good meat, and I didn't want it to go to waste. It was sad to watch this farm end. Your parents had it running beautifully, so productive."

Archangel Gabriel approaches the fire and sits on a log, draping their long light-blue gown neatly over their legs. "Why didn't you take over the farm and make it your own, seeing as you've been living here in the woods around it?"

A frown pinches my forehead as I ponder the idea. "I agree. Nobody was using it, and no one else is going to come here. You should've made it your own."

Yves pauses his chewing and contemplates.

"What is it?" I ask.

His shoulders slump, and he swallows slowly. "I feel as though it's my fault."

Resting my arm on my knee, I gaze at him strangely. "What is?"

He sits in silence, staring into the fire, his distressed face lit by its bright flames.

"Oh, don't make us wait for it, sweetie." Archangel Gabriel leans toward the fire, their pale-blue gown rubbing against the long grass. "The suspense is killing me. Don't make me come and read your mind."

Yves's eyes flash up to Archangel Gabriel, and a pained shock fills them. "You can do that?"

Archangel Gabriel lets out an exaggerated sigh. "Naturally, sweetie. I'm an archangel."

"Have you done it to me already?" Yves genuinely looks concerned.

"Of course, I haven't. You would know if I did. I have to place my palm on your forehead to be able to do that. Besides, it's not something I like to do. It seems rather intrusive finding out everyone's secrets within a few seconds of meeting them." The archangel shakes as though a chill ran down their spine. "I only do it when I have to."

"That's a relief, kind of." Yves's eyes dart to the side, and he sits quietly with a weird look on his face, staring blankly into the fire.

Archangel Gabriel looks to be growing increasingly impatient, reflecting my thoughts. The suspense is getting to me and putting me off my meal.

After a long exhale, Yves's shoulders slump farther, and his face takes on a look of defeat. "I've been living out here since before your parents came and built their cottage. I was hiding in the forest away from people. Nobody wants to live near a person with a tic. They look at me as an outcast, even my own kind—the shape-shifters and witches. They couldn't get rid of me quick enough. They made me so unwelcome that I felt more at home among the trees, with real birds and wildlife. To be honest, I enjoy the peace, but at times, it gets rather lonely." Yves picks up a stick and pokes at the fire. Hot embers flitter into the air. "It was by chance that your parents chose to clear this spot and start their home."

The stick catches alight and breaks off as Yves pokes the coals some more. He throws the remaining length into the flames then rubs the tops of his thighs. "Initially, I watched them from a distance—observing their day-to-day activities unbeknownst to them."

He holds up a hand, as though reading my thoughts. "Yes, I realize this is a form of stalking, but I hadn't seen people in so long that I watched their movements with fascination. Their mundane lives were quite interesting to me. I watched as the little farm grew, and so did your mother's belly. I found their continuous love endearing. They were forever in each other's embrace. They rarely left the farm, and never did I see anyone come and visit." He holds up a finger. "Except for one man. He looked to be about the same age as your father, but he appeared to be human." He frowns. "It was strange to see him with a friend."

"Did you know his name?" I ask.

He tilts his head. "I think it started with a P."

"Piers?"

His eyes brighten. "Yes. That's it. How'd you know?"

"He was my human guardian after my parents were murdered."

"Oh. I'm glad your father knew him, then." His eyes meet mine, and a guilty look passes over his face. "Your parents' love for each other and how they lived was contagious, and I started to fall in love with them from a distance. After a long time, I decided to risk it and fly down and introduce myself."

A strange expression passes through his eyes as his head jerks with tics. "Your mother was still heavily pregnant at the time. I must've given her a shock when I came down. I was already an old man, and I was naked when I landed. My clothes had long since deteriorated. I hadn't shifted into human form for so long, I'd forgotten about etiquette." He looks slightly embarrassed. "She didn't scream or run because she was heavily pregnant. Instead, she faced up to me, strong and determined." One side of his mouth lifts in a smirk. "She cast spell after spell at me. Ones that stunned and ones that made my knees buckle. I landed face-first in the dirt, crumpled in a heap. Thankfully, she held some form of pity for me and didn't throw any painful curses. I asked her later why she didn't attack, and she said she was giving me a chance to prove myself one way or the other."

Half my mouth lifts in a smile. "Didn't you throw any curses at her?"

Yves's eyes widen with horror. "I didn't want to hurt her. You've seen how my magic works."

I nod. "Yes, I have. Good choice." Hearing that my mother didn't throw any painful curses brings me an understanding of why I'm more likely to give people a chance. "Did you ever think she was casting those spells not because she was shocked at your appearance and the fact that you were an old man, but because they hadn't seen anybody in ages and were in hiding? They probably didn't know you'd been watching them for years as a crow."

He shrugs. "Those could also be reasons, but your mother was a stunning woman. I was an old man, and it's not the best look to be naked in front of a beautiful woman." He pauses for a minute. "After throwing several curses at me, including ones that stopped me from speaking, she finally released my voice box, and I managed to hold up my hand, begging her to stop. She did."

His head tics again. "When she stopped attacking me, I explained that I came to introduce myself. I explained that I was a shape-shifter and kind of a wizard and I meant no harm." He kicked his feet into the loose dirt in front of him. "She just stared at me, stunned, but she didn't stop me from speaking again. Instead, she remained silent and listened as I attempted to prove myself and tell her my story."

He kicked the dirt harder, and some loose granules landed in the fire. "I explained how I was alone and how I had stumbled across the cottage. I lied a little bit so I didn't seem like a genuine stalker. She looked skeptical, so I changed into a crow right in front of her."

After a pause, I ask, "And what did she do?"

"She raised an eyebrow then asked, "Are you the crow that's been hanging around for years? The one that sits and watches our livestock from the post and seems to be watching our house at times?" He huffs at the thought. "She was a smart woman, your mother. Very observant. Because of that, I told her the truth—the full truth. Surprisingly, she let me stay. She fed me and gave me some clothes from her husband's cupboard so I wouldn't disgrace her anymore.

"She often invited me into their home, sharing their food with me. Your father was also welcoming once he met me. They treated me like a friend. They let me use their bath out in the open, allowing me to clean myself. Your mother made me gowns that I hid in the forest and used when I changed into a human. In fact, she made this gown for me, which is why it's torn in so many spots." He pulled at the black fabric, showing some of the worn parts.

The story touched my heart, but it also raised more questions. "So, how were you part of the reason for their deaths?"

His eyes fill with earnestness. "When you were born, I held you and played with you. I used to shape-shift to a crow, and you would come find me. And when I was a human and cloaked, I would hold you in my arms. At times, when you wouldn't stop crying, I would take you from your mother and entertain you for a while to let her have a break. Not that you were a terrible baby. It's just that all babes drive their mothers crazy at times. Your father was also a great help with you when you were young. Don't think I was taking his place. It's just that he would often be out in the fields tending to the animals on the farm, so I would help your mother. I would also look after you so your mother could help your father in the fields. I was happy to help, and in return, they made sure I was never hungry."

The tormented look flashes over his face again. "They ignored all my tics and my unusual traits. I knew their secret of being a witch and a shape-shifter, and I didn't care. Perhaps because of that, they also accepted me as I was. It took years, but the acceptance gave me the courage to start traveling back to civilized areas again. My trips became farther and covered a wider area. At each new village I entered, I tried to buy items or partake in their festivals. Each time I was shunned, and I would return to the farm and be surrounded by love. It gave me the courage to try again in a different village."

I couldn't help thinking this was either crazy or gutsy. "Why would you keep searching for villages if they gave you a bad reception each time?"

He shakes his head. "I don't know. I guess it was because your parents made me feel so loved that I thought there was still hope out there, that perhaps the world had changed since I became a hermit, but this was not the case."

He sits in silence for a while, his face distant and filled with thought. He picks up a stick near him and slowly peels off layers of bark. "At one stage, I landed in a small village and discovered that it consisted entirely of shape-shifters. I had hopes for this village, and I befriended a child there. He was about ten, and I believe the young are more open-minded and less tarnished than the parents." He tosses the shredded stick aside. "I was ecstatic when he decided to befriend me. I visited regularly. It was a long flight from the farm to this village, but I would go, keen for new friends."

He runs a hand through his hair. It gets stuck in the tangled mess, and he struggles to free his fingers. "During one of the many visits, the boy asked me where I came from and where I lived, and I gave him some information. I told him who I lived with, thinking it would mean nothing to say their first names. I mentioned that they had an adorable baby girl with eyes the purist of green and blond hair just like her father. I didn't think anything of it. Every time I visited the young boy, he would casually ask questions about my home and the people I lived with. He never asked anything too intense. Eventually, he asked which direction I came from and how far I traveled. The questions seemed innocent, stemming from genuine curiosity about how I got around and the effort I took to see him."

Yves clasps his hands together and squashes them between his knees. "I told him, glad that someone took an interest in me. I thought he was purely interested in me." He lets out a long breath.

"I knew him for six months, but just a couple of weeks after I told him where I lived, people turned up on your parents' doorstep. They were shape-shifters. I didn't know their names. At first, your parents hesitantly welcomed them into their home. I watched from a distance." He gives me a pointed look. "Eventually, the conversation turned into an argument. I never went inside the house. I was outside listening with my crow hearing. It sounded like they were trying to break your parents up as well as telling them to kill you. Your parents wouldn't. They had been living peacefully in this area for so long and loved you dearly."

He rises to his feet and paces, his tic working overtime. "After a while, the people departed—leaving your parents safe but disturbed. Piers came to visit a few days afterward. He stayed a few nights, which I thought was strange, and he seemed to be spending a lot of time with you."

A deep sadness fills Yves's eyes as he looks at me. "Now that I know he was your guardian, it explains so much. They must have been preparing. I didn't visit your parents when he was there. Instead, I went for another one of my trips, and when I returned, it was a gruesome mess. The cottage was in disarray. Your parents' bodies lay bloodied inside their little cottage. I wept for weeks, if not months, and I have mourned and lived in this forest without visiting anyone ever since." He sits and kicks at the dirt before plunking his head in his hands.

Archangel Gabriel places a comforting hand on his shoulder, and Yves flinches, as if not used to contact.

"I don't know who did it. I don't know who came here and killed them. I don't know if it was that group that came here or someone they told, but it still feels as though it was my fault. Even if it was, there was nothing I could do. I was merely an old man and a crow. I have no fighting skills, no strength, and my wizard powers leave a lot to be desired. The worst I could do would be to pick the meat from the murderers' dying flesh. That would be satisfying, if I had the opportunity to do so."

He looks at me, his eyes full of pain. "I looked for you. I had grown quite fond of you, but I couldn't see any signs of you. I thought perhaps you were part of the massacre or maybe they had taken you elsewhere to kill you. I didn't know where you were." His head tics uncontrollably, and he rests it on his knees, hiding his face behind crossed arms. "I'm a coward." His voice is muffled. "I should have pursued it harder and avenged your parents. After everything they did for me, I did nothing in return. That's one of the reasons I followed you to the witches. I wanted to make up for my inadequacies."

I rise to my feet and place a hand on his arm. "You buried my parents, didn't you?"

He nods.

"Then, as an old man, you did as much as you could."

Archangel Gabriel stands next to me, their face full of compassion as they gaze at the crumpled Yves. "That's a terrible story, sweetie. Are the people who came to the cottage that day still alive?"

Yves shrugs. "I don't know."

Archangel Gabriel places their hands on their hips. "Okay, then. May I read your mind? I might be able to get an image of where the town was that you visited and get a picture of the people and the young boy that you trusted."

Yves gazes up at Archangel Gabriel with shock in his eyes then slowly nods. "If this will help get revenge for Ava's parents, then please do. I honestly did love them."

Without wasting a moment, Archangel Gabriel places a palm on Yves's forehead. A small white light shines out of their palm into Yves's forehead, and the archangel gazes deep into the man's faded eyes. It takes a few moments before they pull their palm away. "Right. I have a good picture of these people in my mind." They turn to me. "I'm coming with you back to the shape-shifters' village. I'm going to help you find them."

CHAPTER TWENTY-TWO

"Where did they go?"

I crack my eyes open, my vision hazy as I rub the sleep from them.

Yves paces, his eyes darting everywhere, his tic working overtime. His worn black gown swishes against his legs with the rapid movement.

Stretching my arms above my head, I yawn before climbing to my feet to get a better view of the paddocks.

Half-heartedly, I search the fields overgrown with weeds and grass. I'm not expecting to find them. "I don't know, but don't stress. Archangels go many places. They have many responsibilities." I shrug. To be honest, I'm not surprised Archangel Gabriel is gone. Trying to calm Yves, I place a hand on his shoulder. "I'm not worried. They always come back when they've finished. Never have they left me stranded."

I return to the firepit and sit on a large stone, eating

my meager breakfast of dried fruit and nuts. Black ashes are all that remain of the fire from last night. "I'm going to head off anyway. I don't need to wait for Archangel Gabriel. They'll find me when they want to."

"But you don't know where to go." Yves approaches and grabs a handful of my dried fruit and nuts from the leather bag, tossing them into his mouth. A sadness lies in his eyes. I'm not sure if it's because he's stirred memories from the past or because I'm leaving.

I stare at him. "But you do."

"I do?" He stops chewing, and his jaw drops in shock, exposing the remaining food in his mouth.

"Of course, you do. Just take me back to the spot where you met the young boy. That will be the beginning of the search."

His eyes dart in different directions, looking panicked. "My recollection is foggy. It was so many years ago. My memory is old, and I'm sure the path has changed with growth or development." He shakes his head, and his shoulders slump. "I'm not much help. My usual story."

I offer him some more of my nut mix, and he shakes his head. "That's okay. We'll work it out. You can change into a crow, and I'll follow you. I'll ride my broomstick, though, as I want to take my things with me."

"I'll even carry your clothes for you," I smirk. "Like my mother, I prefer you clothed."

He chuckles then snorts. "I prefer me clothed too. Okay. I'll do my best to show you the way."

I pack up my things and throw them into my bag, then unclip my hairpin and straighten the pin into one length. Immediately it grows into the broomstick.

"That is a rather special pin you have there." Yves's eyes widen. "I saw you do that before I met you, but it hasn't grown old. I could watch that process over and over. You've definitely inherited your mother's traits of a witch. She was a very talented witch. Who taught you how to do that?"

"No one taught me the ways of witches. My guardians were humans, and they didn't take me to any shape-shifters or witches. I stumbled across everything myself, whether it was embedded deep in a memory or whether I just managed to concoct the spells. I've written everything I know in my books." I dip my hand in my leather bag and retrieve one of the miniaturized spell books. I whisper a spell, and the book grows to its normal size on the palm of my hand.

Yves reaches for the book, and I allow him to take it. He attempts to open it without success.

I smile. "You won't get it open. My books are charmed shut." My smirk grows wider. "Not even an archangel can open them."

His eyes flick up to me, then he giggles and snorts. "Now, that I would like to see."

I chuckle with him. "It's quite hilarious, actually."

He tries to open the book again.

"I must leave it that way because these are only for certain witches and shape-shifters' eyes. I must protect these spells at all costs and make sure they don't get into the wrong hands. If they did, they could do a lot of damage."

He hands me back the book. "I understand. You have a good head on you. That's very clever thinking. I should've been like that when I betrayed your parents' whereabouts."

After minimizing the book, I pack it away and place a hand on his shoulder. "It's not your fault that you were naive. I understand what you were going through, wanting to be with someone and have more friends. It's kind of the way I feel about wanting to have family members. I came back so I could meet my family, get to know them, and hopefully have more people around. Like you, I'm all alone except for the archangels. Everyone on this earth that I've cared about has been killed. This adventure is critical to me."

"Then we must go." He shape-shifts before my eyes. His crow form flies out of his crumpled pile of clothes, and I gather them up, placing them in my bag. Sitting on my broom, I follow as he flies in the opposite direction of the witches.

WE FLY FOR MOST OF THE DAY, SUDDENLY STOPPING WHEN Yves lands and changes back into his human form. I land beside him, reaching into the bag and throwing him his gown with my head turned away. When the rustling of clothes quiets, I turn to him. He groans, sounding frustrated, and he paces while wringing his hands.

"What's wrong?" I ask.

"I can't remember the way. I feel like I'm leading us along the wrong path."

"What makes you say that?"

"Nothing looks the same. I've flown in my crow form, trying to go the way I traveled back then, but nothing is as I remember. It all looks so different. I haven't traveled this path for nearly as long as you've been alive. Things have grown and changed." He paces, and I watch him go back and forth between the trees, looking extremely frustrated.

"You're stressing way too much. Why don't you relax and catch your breath?"

He shakes his head. "I want to get you there as soon as possible. I want you to have your answers. I feel like I owe you that."

"We don't have to get there in one day." I stand in his path and face him, making him look at me. "We'll get there. If you can't remember, Archangel Gabriel will be back soon. They can lead us in the right direction. If they have to, they can read your mind and watch your memory. Even if you can't remember, they can still access it."

Blue particles form on my right, and I look in time to see it develop into Archangel Gabriel.

"Hello, sweeties. Did someone mention my name?" They chuckle.

"Oh, thank god!" Yves exclaims.

"Now, now. No need to be blasphemous." The archangel waggles their finger at Yves.

"We were talking about you," I say.

The archangel clasps their hands together. "I thought my ears were tingling."

I raise an eyebrow. "Do you know when we talk about you?"

"No. To be honest, I came on a more serious matter. The angels need you, Ava." The archangel reaches for my hand and grips it in theirs.

Yves stares forlornly at us. "Wait. Where are you going?"

"I'm taking Ava to another archangel battle. We need her help with the demons."

"But what about me? What am I to do?"

I squeeze his hand gently. "Wait here. Catch some food. I'll be back soon, and we'll finish our journey. Okay?"

His head jerks up and down swiftly, and at that moment, I dissipate. My body transforms into tiny particles and reforms in the middle of the bloody archangel-versus-demon battle. The second I feel all my cells regroup, I begin my transformation into a dragon.

My blood burns hot, and my belly brews the furnace of my dragon fire. Green scales push forth out of my skin, and my arms and legs thicken to hold my expanding torso. Sharp, mirroring pains shoot through my shoulder blades as my green membrane wings grow from my back.

When the pain subsides, I know my dragon trans-formation is complete. I stomp all four feet on the ground and release a brilliant roar. I'm so ready for this fight. This is just what I need to work out the frustration of not finding my parents' betrayer or murderers.

At the end of my roar, a plume of fire shoots out of my mouth, and I aim it at the sky, careful not to hit the archangels. Assessing the area, I brace myself, ready to push off into the sky. I unfurl my long green wings and arch them as I squat, preparing for the takeoff.

Something wraps around my forelegs and tightens quickly, pulling them together. It knocks me off balance, and I fall to the ground, chest-first. Ready to defend myself, I breathe in deeply and prepare to exhale a large plume of fire when something tightens around my muzzle. Eyes wide, I stare at the rope securing my jaw shut.

Twisting, I gaze at my feet. They're bound together. It's no wonder I collapsed. I groan, and steam shoots out of my nose as I lose myself in shock. I don't under-stand what's going on. My eyes dart in all different directions, looking for the cause of these events. The archangels fight the demons, and I can see them scat-tered in the distance, including the pale-blue form of Archangel Gabriel. The blue-gowned archangel spins around, circled by demons, and releases several shuriken, their aim true. As soon as the flying stars hit the demons, the demons disintegrate to dust and sprinkle the ground. Archangel Gabriel reaches out a hand toward the released stars, as though beckoning them to return, and they listen to the command. The archangel throws another round at the approaching demons.

I call, but my roar is muffled, muzzled by the rope. Even if I could roar, I doubt the archangels would pay me any attention, as they are distracted by the demons surrounding them. They are so used to me being able to defend myself that they aren't worried about me. Even I'm in shock over my predicament. Never have I known the demons to act in a concerted attack.

Something catches my eye, and I glance in that direction. A dark hole springs up in the middle of the field, not far from where I am. The gatekeeper lurks within its reach, ready to take off into the shadows again, running away like a coward, leaving behind the demons. He cackles, sending shivers down my spine. A laugh is supposed to be a pleasant sound, but his is not. Pure evil fills the noise, and if I had hairs right now, I know they would all be standing on end. Instead, my scales prickle, even the ones that rest against the ground holding my weight. I am disgusted by the sound. I've heard that this is a call, and I wonder who the gate-keeper is calling.

I pull my eyes away from him, searching the area. Several demons surround me, looking lost yet pleased that my snout is restrained and not breathing fire. They throw black pulses at me, which rebound off my scales. I breathe a sigh of relief, thankful for my scales' resilience, even to the demonic black pulses. I wonder if this is a typical dragon trait or if it's because I'm a witch as well, which magically enhances my scales for protection.

The demons draw together when they realize their pulses aren't getting through, and it surprises me, setting me on edge. They seem to be adapting, and hundreds of them come together, gathering around the ends of the ropes. They plant their feet against the earth and pull. I slide the tiniest amount. They do it again, hunkering their little legs against my dragon form and pulling in unison. They do this several times before it sinks in that they're pulling me toward the portal. The gatekeeper cackles in the corner with each progression.

Again, I attempt to open my mouth and fail—the restriction of the rope disables me from calling for help. I can't roar, and I can't climb to my feet. Remembering my tail, I slash it down, thumping it against the ground. I'm not sure if the ground moved with the force of the thump or if the power projected my body slightly. I thump some more, aiming for the demons, and watch as they scatter. Hope makes my heart skip a beat. Then I watch in horror as the demons run to a farther spot on the rope beyond the reach of my tail—a move that squashes my small success.

My mind races, desperate for my next move—I must get out of this somehow. The demons pull again, and I inch toward the portal. With wide eyes, I observe its size and almost laugh to myself. I'm too big to fit. The demons aren't going to be able to pull me though that tiny hole.

The gatekeeper raises his hands, as though reading my thoughts, and the portal grows.

CHAPTER TWENTY-THREE

Thrashing my tail and using my great wings, I manage to twist my body around and retrieve some ground, but the demons continue to pull. If I'm not careful, they could use my body's elevation to draw me closer to the portal. Despite my struggle, they drag me toward the portal, inch by inch. My heart rate rises, panic gripping me with each inch that disappears. With each piece of ground I lose, the gatekeeper cackles more. If I didn't despise him enough before, I hate him now. Only an evil man would relish someone else's fall.

The demons continue to pull, and the end of my legs enter the portal. My talons retract in shock when they feel the evil on the other side. I search for an archangel to help, yet all I find is destruction. It's no wonder they aren't coming to my rescue when so many angels are falling. Many of them I don't know personally. Even so, my heart cries for them. There are so few angels already, and any loss is devastating.

The demons' possession of me stops right now. They can't hold me like this. I must help—not only for myself but also for the archangels. I have nothing to live for, but they have everything. The angels are the protectors of the world, and it's the world we're attempting to protect from this demon invasion.

Determination shoots through my body, and the simplest answer suddenly occurs to me. It's so basic that I have no idea why I couldn't think of it before. The risk I perceive is worth it. With another yank, my legs are pulled farther into the portal, and the evil creeps up my bones. It's now or never to execute my idea.

I shift, my heart rejoicing as the particles separate and reform. The ropes that bound the dragon aren't enchanted like the chains at the witches' coven. The demons probably don't know how to enchant them. As my dragon form dissipates, my human witch forms, and I stand in the middle of the battlefield dressed only in my shape-shifting underwear.

Distracted by the maneuver I made, the demons stand, blank faced, holding empty ropes. Judging by the demons' reactions, they didn't know I had that ability. With this form, I bring the anger of my dragon. My belly roars with frustration and irritation over the deaths of the angels. The worthless killings and destruction infuriate me, as does how the gatekeeper and the demons continue to attack the people and defenders of Earth.

Grabbing hold of this anger and frustration, I let it twirl in my stomach. I allow it to gather and build and bring me the much-needed energy I'm about to use. I haven't fought the demons in this form, and I'm about to find out what I can do to them with my witch powers. Some say witches are part demon—I'm about to find out. The energy inside me has built to capacity, leaving no room for anything else.

I cast my hands wide, clasping my energy and grabbing hold of every weapon within the vicinity. I can feel the traces of angelic power attached to each weapon that the angels hold, blessed by an archangel, some of them probably blessed by Zacharias. I push aside thoughts of him because the distraction will only bring me sadness. I focus the angelic power given to these blades, spinning their points toward each demon that is within the vicinity of the weapon, and I rip them from the archangels' hands straight into the demons' hearts. The bodies of the demons disintegrate and scatter to the ground—the weapons land in the dust.

The archangels, stripped of their weapons, stand openmouthed, glaring at the spot where the demons once stood. Confusion creases their faces, yet they don't hover, trying to understand the outcome. Instead, they dive for their weapons and search for the nearest demon. The fight must continue. Many archangels have already fallen, and they must leap over their fellow angels' bodies to reach the next demon in line. Only three heads turn my way, Archangels Michael, Raphael, and Gabriel. The creative angel grins with mischief and pride as they catch each returning shuriken.

Archangel Michael approaches, his sword dripping

dark demon blood. Black splatters his golden breast-plate. "Thank you, Ava. I see you're just as powerful in your witch form as you are in your dragon form to these demons. Keep up the good work."

My chest swells with pride. "After everything the gatekeeper and demons have done to me, my loved ones, and Zacharias, it's my pleasure to help." I spin, looking for the gatekeeper and his portal. It's disappeared—typical of the gatekeeper when things get tough. When he's threatened, he retreats to another dimension. Where exactly, I don't know. All I know is that he manages to do it quickly.

At this point, I'm not too worried about where he goes. I don't have any loved ones he can reach. Zacharias is untouchable, even if the gatekeeper knows where he is. I have no one else I'm close to at present. Everything has been stripped from me, thanks to the gatekeeper. I can look for him later in life.

Archangel Michael turns from me to fight again. Archangel Raphael, the healing angel, nods at me in appreciation then turns to the nearest archangel to see if he can heal them. There are endless bodies, so many of them lying still.

Demons no longer plague me, so I concentrate on building my power again, winding it up within my torso, and strip the archangels momentarily of their weapons, thrusting them into the closest demons' hearts. Again, every demon fighting an archangel is pierced by the angelically blessed weapons and falls to the ground. Archangel Gabriel is surrounded by many piles of dust, each mound topped with a shuriken.

The remaining demons are wrought with confusion. They have seen the others fall to an invisible opponent, and they don't know where to look. It's apparent they haven't come across a foe like this before, and worry riddles their ugly faces. Their bulging eyes dart from place to place in search of their unseen adversary.

The archangels scoop their weapons from the piles of dust and pursue the demons. The remaining demons take one look at them, and their bulging eyes expand, fear overwhelming their pale, shriveled faces. Frantic, they search for the gatekeeper's portal only to realize he's no longer there to collect them—any search for another escape proves fruitless. Out of desperation, they throw black pulses, which the angels dodge easily.

The tides have turned, and it's no longer the archangels falling, but the demons. If the demons weren't so evil, I would feel sorry for them for being pursued by strong archangels until every last one has fallen.

I continue the battle in my human form, finding it as powerful as my dragon. In witch form, my body is more susceptible to injury, but my powers are just as strong, if not stronger. My witch power achieves great things.

With the threat gone, Archangel Michael approaches me. "Thank you again for your help, Ava."

"As always, I'm willing to help, especially in battles against the gatekeeper. We wondered where Archangel

Gabriel disappeared to. One day they were with us, and the next day, we woke to find them gone."

Archangel Gabriel's chuckle reaches me from behind. "Ah, yes. Sorry about that, sweetie. Archangel Michael called me in the middle of the night, and I didn't want to wake you."

I smile at them. "I wasn't worried. I figured you'd be back at one point or another. You did give Yves a scare, though. If you're finished here, we could use your help. Yves doesn't know where to go. He's tried but hasn't quite hit the mark. We're stuck in the middle of the forest somewhere and don't know which way to turn. If I could read his mind like you, then I would be able to know where he went all those years ago."

"Hmm." The archangel props up their chin with a hand. "Maybe we can work on that. You may have a power in there somewhere that'll help you read memories."

I beam. I'm sure other witches don't have that gift. "You have no idea how much I'd love that." I extend my hand. "Shall we?" The creative archangel clasps my hand, and we teleport back to Yves.

CHAPTER TWENTY-FOUR

"Where is he?" A frown creases Archangel Gabriel's forehead while they search through the tree trunks.

"I don't know. This is where I left him. I'm certain." I indicate my backpack lying against a tree.

Together we search through the trees, finding his clothes in a crumpled heap on the ground. My search continues in the tops of the trees as I look for a crow. "Perhaps he got bored and took flight."

A low grumble sounds behind me. I pivot, spotting a large bear shadowing us. It growls, low and menacing, as it stalks forward one paw at a time. The smell of churned-up mud and crumpled leaves fills my nose as I take a deep breath, composing my nerves. It must've trampled this area several times looking for Yves. I hope he's okay. I hope the bear hasn't eaten him. My eyes instinctively dart to the ground, observing the paw prints through the dirt. Thankfully, I don't see any sign of blood or feathers.

The bear growls again, its speed increasing as it heads my way. I prepare to turn into the same shape. I don't want to hurt the bear. It's probably only hunting for food or protecting its young. Which it is doing doesn't matter.

Concentrating on the form, I feel my particles start to separate when I see a blue flash dash in between the bear and me. I pause my transformation and watch. Archangel Gabriel stands before me, calmness radiating off them, reminding me of the time when Zacharias did the same thing to a wolf. The bear balks, watching them.

Slowly, Archangel Gabriel approaches the bear. "Now, now, sweet bear. You don't want to attack us. We aren't a threat to you. We're merely looking for a friend, then we'll be on our way." The bear doesn't move. The only improvement is the dulling of its aggression.

A crow calls in the distance. The bear glances up, irritation in its eyes.

I wonder what Yves did to the bear to agitate it. The bear stomps forward again, and Archangel Gabriel holds up a hand.

"Now, now. They're just staying safe from you. The crow didn't mean any harm." The peaceful archangel continues to talk to the bear in a low, calming voice.

The bear halts, distracted by Archangel Gabriel as they tentatively approach it, their arms remaining outstretched.

The bear calms as the archangel continues to speak in a soft voice, placing a hand close to its snout. The bear breathes it in. Its large nostrils suck in the scent, and its eyes widen as the realization hits it that Archangel Gabriel isn't human but an angelic being. It drops to its haunches and sits placidly, allowing Archangel Gabriel to pet its head.

"There. That's a nice bear. See? We're not coming to hurt you. We're just passing through. You're safe with us."

The bear rubs its head affectionately against Archangel Gabriel, playfulness replacing the harshness in its eyes.

Archangel Gabriel scratches it under its chin and around his chest, then playfully pushes it over and rubs the bear under its arms. The bear wrestles back as Archangel Gabriel straddles it, and they roll around, teasing each other like a couple of cubs.

I'm awed by the sight and enjoy the spectacle, almost jealous, wishing I could join in. The bear and Archangel Gabriel topple head over heels in all different directions, the archangel laughing with pleasure. The bear lets out a groan, the sound no longer angry or aggressive. Their joy is contagious, and I can't help smiling.

Yves flies down and transforms into a human, grabbing his clothes and ducking behind a tree to change. When dressed, he comes around and watches Archangel Gabriel playing with the bear. "Caw. If only I could've done that. That thing tried to kill me. I did the whole crouching down, submissive thing, and it still went after me. I was lucky to escape with the feathers on my back."

Glancing at the bear, I chuckle. "I don't know what you're talking about. He's so placid. Look! He only wants to play."

The side-eye he gives me shows he's unimpressed.

Archangel Gabriel spins around with the bear a little more before rolling to a stand. They pet the bear on the head. "Okay, so we've had our fun. It's time for us to go. Take care, beautiful bear." The bear nudges the archangel's hand affectionately then turns around and strolls off into the forest.

"I wish I knew how you do that," I say to Archangel Gabriel.

They shrug. "It's just an angel thing. The bears know that the angels are guardians and we're not here to hurt them, so they let us do whatever once they realize what we are. I don't know that it's something humans can do unless the bears already know them. It's just the way it is." The archangel gazes at Yves. "Ah. There you are. We thought we'd lost you."

"I had to run from the bear. It was vicious. I was lucky to get away." He eyes the archangel suspiciously. "Although looking at you playing with the bear, you would never know."

Archangel Gabriel grins and places a hand on Yves's shoulder. "Don't take it to heart. Even Ava can't do that." The archangel looks at me then at Yves. "I hope you don't mind, but I need to teach Ava how to read minds. I heard you can't remember the directions to where the shape-shifter you knew lived."

Yves looks at me uncertainly. "Yes, that's right. Is Ava able to do that?"

"I think she will be able to." Archangel Gabriel's crystal-blue eyes study me intensely. "She has many gifts that a normal witch doesn't have." They stand back, cock a hip to the side, and cross their arms with one hand balancing their chin, looking deep in thought. "Hm. What's the best way to do this?"

After a moment, their eyes light up. "Ah, I know." They approach me. "First, I'm going to show you rather than tell you. I think that's the best way. To do this, I'm going to have to inject the information through my hand into your forehead."

Fear creeps its ugly tentacles into me, threatening to take control. I push it aside and nod apprehensively. "Okay. Let's do this." Besides my trepidation, I am very keen to learn this gift, and I trust Archangel Gabriel wholly.

They place a hand on my forehead, and I take a shaky breath. Within seconds, visions inundate my head with instructions. It's so clear and precise that I know I won't have to ask any questions. The rush is incredible, and I wonder if this euphoria I feel is what it's like to be an angel. Or is it only a feeling they get when they receive new information on how to help people do things?

Following my visual instructions, I place my hand on Yves's forehead. His brown eyes cloud with concern, and the wrinkles deepen around his eyes. Still, he faces his fears and allows me to continue. It's an effort to reach his forehead, requiring me to stand on my tiptoes and bring my ear close to his heart. His heart thumps rapidly. I want to tell him everything will be okay, but I can't guarantee it when I've never done this before. Despite having instructions from Archangel Gabriel, I may do something incorrectly.

Abolishing the thought, I instill confidence in myself. I've received clear step-by-step instructions. I can do this. Summoning my witch's power, I let it sit, whirring, waiting for the next step. Yves's eyes don't leave me, and I release my power into his brain and his memory.

He gasps, and I almost pull away, thinking I might be hurting him. Then I realize it's the shock of the intrusion. He doesn't retreat, giving in to the invasion. This troubles me slightly. After everything he's been through, he still trusts me, even though he doesn't know me well.

The first thing I notice is his pure heart. He doesn't mean anybody harm. What he told me at my parents' house was the truth. He's a loner. He has no one in his life except for the few interactions with my parents and myself and the one shape-shifter that he trusted those many years ago. It doesn't take long to come across the spot in his life where he interacted with other people in a different town. It's the weirdest feeling, fast-forwarding through someone's life to get to a specific spot. I don't see all of it, but I catch glimpses, getting the gist of what's going on.

As I go through his introduction to this one boy, I gasp when I hear the name. I can't believe what I'm hearing, and I want to make sure it's the same person. I study the features intensely, looking at everything that defines his face. The telltale features are there, confirming he's the person I think he is. The face is the same, yet wrinkle-free and much younger. I don't want to believe it, but the evidence is right there in front of me. Not only that, when I retrace the flight path to the town, I confirm it's the town where my shape-shifter family lives. I know the man displayed in front of me as a boy. I met him at Vezelay. It pains me, but it's true. By the set of his eyes and the dimple in his chin, it's Andre.

CHAPTER TWENTY-FIVE

I t's a struggle to force away the shock so I can investigate without any bias, pushing forward to when Theodore turns up at my parents' farm along with other people. My uncle Theodore, of all people. Sadness sinks to the bottom of my stomach. Not only is the boy Andre, but his father is one of the shape-shifters who visited the farm. I study each face, trying to see if I know them. There are still many people I haven't met from the shape-shifter village. On top of that, most of the people aren't facing the crow, and Yves doesn't fly to a different position to get a better look. I guess he didn't see the need. As far as he knew, they were random visitors.

One of the women turns around, and I concentrate on her face. There's something familiar about her. It's only vague. The woman looks from my parents to someone in the group with them. When she looks at my parents, one side of her mouth lifts, not in a smile, more like a look of disappointment. A large dimple briefly forms on one cheek. I frown. There is definitely something familiar about her. I just can't place it. While keeping my mind ticking over who she may be, I move my attention to the rest of the group.

From Yves's crow perspective, I watch the argument through the window. Only hearing snippets of the conversation, it's difficult to make out what's going on, but one thing is clear. They've discovered my parents' farm. When the turmoil subsides, the people leave angry, my parents remain unharmed, and the mystery woman stays unsolved.

Not long after the group leaves, a distressed Yves visits my parents, admitting his error from the beginning. I'm surprised yet also proud that my parents don't treat him any differently. They also know he didn't intend them any harm. They knew he was a loner seeking other people's approval. Yet sadness squashes the pride I hold. Little did they know that this would lead to their deaths.

My hand remains over his forehead, and I stare into his deep brown eyes. One part of me wants to go to the time when he found my parents murdered, and the other part doesn't. The mere thought drags me through a pit of sadness. Despite this, my curiosity takes over, and I skim to the spot where Yves returns to the farm. I relive his reaction and feel his devastation as he spots my murdered parents. The guilt pours out of every one of his pores. The emotion almost wipes me from my feet. I know he's telling the truth. Their murder completely shattered him, and the guilt tripled because he blames himself. The devastation and guilt are so intense I have trouble standing. My legs want to buckle from the weakness and devastation.

I push on, following his steps into the house and watch through vision blurred with tears as he buries them. My knees burn as Yves's knees collide with the rocks at the foot of their fresh graves. After seeing this, there's no doubt in my mind that he didn't intend for any of this to happen. It's a series of unfortunate events set into motion purely by accident. One small act of desperation to have friends destroyed his only true friends.

My free hand braces his shoulder as I attempt to stabilize us from the intensity of the emotion. Both of us have dealt with every single emotion that he felt at the time. I pause my investigation and slowly pull my hand away from his forehead. His eyes are troubled, but they soften after the shock disintegrates.

I squeeze his upper arm. "Thank you, Yves. Thank you for your cooperation." He briefly wobbles when I remove my hand from his shoulder then steadies himself and stands straighter.

Archangel Gabriel hugs me around my shoulders. "Did it work, sweetie? You look as though it worked. Both of you look stunned."

I nod jerkily. "Yes, it did, and I believe I know the man who used to be his friend."

Yves and Archangel Gabriel look at me, their faces shocked.

I continue. "The town Yves visited is the shape-shifter village—the one where my father grew up. It's just sheer bad luck that Yves stumbled across Vezelay. He had no idea it was my father's old town."

The weight of the circumstances droops my shoulders, and I gaze at the ground. "This is why the betrayal happened, because many people in his village were looking for my parents in the first place." Intently, I gaze at Yves. "It's not your fault, though. Don't feel guilty. You had no intention to harm them and couldn't have known. Your friend didn't give you any indication that they knew who my father was. Whether it was intentional or purely because the person was young, I don't know."

"Do you know where you need to go, sweetie?" Archangel Gabriel asks.

"Yes, I do. I'm not sure exactly how to pursue it from here, but I do know where I need to go. I can work it out from here."

Archangel Gabriel places an arm around my shoulders again and hugs me tight. "That's great, sweetie. I'll let you go this part alone unless you think you need me."

I shake my head. "I know you're busy. I should be fine from here. I'll find my way to the village from this little spot."

A sad smile crosses the archangel's face. "I'm always busy, but if you need me, I'm here."

I shake my head again, rubbing my upper arms, deep in thought. "No. I'll be fine."

They look at me with earnest blue eyes that weigh the options. "I'll still check in on you from time to time."

I nod and smile half-heartedly. "Thank you. I look forward to your visits. You're always wonderful company."

I watch with a sad heart as the androgynous angel dissipates into blue particles then disappears. I don't know what my near future will bring, but I know my parents' betrayal leaves a bitter taste in my mouth. Whether Andre knew he betrayed my parents, or whether he had good intentions, I don't know, but I am about to find out.

CHAPTER TWENTY-SIX

Yves stands stunned, openmouthed and staring at the spot Archangel Gabriel stood only moments before. "I'm sorry. I don't know how I forgot the way. Now that I've watched it with you again, I know I should've remembered. It hasn't been long since I watched it with Archangel Gabriel."

His statement is correct. He should have remembered it. Yet after seeing inside his mind, I have no doubt that he isn't trying to be deceitful. "It's okay. You're getting along in years. Do you even know how old you are?"

He shakes his head, and his tic follows. "I have seen many moons and many cycles of weather. Even so, I've had no way to calculate them. I have no idea. The memory fades as you get older. It's harder to remember things." A sadness crosses his face, and he looks to be chastising himself. He shakes his head. "Even so, I still should've remembered."

I rub his shoulder gently. "Come. We must go."

Slipping my hairpin out of my hair, I unfold it, watching it grow. I never grow tired of watching the process. It leads me to wonder—I have so much more to learn about my witching powers. I've only touched the surface. On top of this, because I keep interesting company, I'm learning abilities that many witches don't know. I must write my new capabilities in my spell book.

Yves dissipates then reforms as a crow. I stoop down and pick up his clothes, packing them into my bag before straddling my broom and flying in the direction of the village. The distance isn't far. The older man's memory wasn't as bad as he thought. He'd just been preoccupied.

We land not far from the village, and I pack up my broom and slide the pin into my hair before tossing Yves's clothes behind me. I make a mental note. As soon as I make some more of my shape-shifting material, I should make him some underwear.

As we approach the village, I try to process how shape-shifters managed to kill a shape-shifter and a witch, both powerful. I can't help thinking there must have been some trickery involved or some sort of weapon to handicap a witch and destabilize a formidable shape-shifter.

A bluebird flutters between the trees, its tiny frame barely standing out, even though it's blue. If I didn't know what I was looking for, I could have missed it.

Not knowing which bluebird it is, I stiffen with antici-pation. I roll my shoulders. Andre could be innocent.

The gust of wind flies through the trees and knocks the bluebird a bit off course, and it struggles to land on a branch. I chuckle and wave to the bluebird. "Why don't you come down and transform? I've brought a friend. We're not here to harm the village."

The bluebird flies to the ground and transforms before our eyes into Yvonne, wearing her shape-shifting underwear. "Ava. So glad to see you. I love these shape-shifting clothes." She runs a hand over the material before her eyes dart warily to Yves. "Who's this?" Her nose screws up with a look of disgust.

Her distrust doesn't surprise me. The bluebirds had a protectiveness of the village instilled into them, and Yves doesn't look like an ordinary human. His clothes are threadbare, and if someone is unfortunate enough to stand downwind, a sour stench of unwashed body assaults them. Yves's tic increases, a sign of his nervousness.

A wave of affection flushes through my heart as I look at the decrepit old man. "This is Yves. I ran across him on my way to the witches. He assisted me in escaping from them."

Even though he wasn't able to do anything benefi-cial, it's not a lie. His attempt to assist me deserves credit.

Yves looks down at his feet and shuffles them. "I wouldn't really call it assistance."

I fix the hood that fell awkwardly off his head. "You

didn't leave me stranded there by myself, and you came to help." I lift his chin with my finger and look directly into his eyes. "In my opinion, that's assistance."

He smiles sheepishly, and I know what he is thinking. I had the discussion earlier with him not to mention the angels to anybody. It's our little secret. Exactly as I asked, he remains tight-lipped, not giving away any other information.

Yvonne observes him with critical eyes then pushes her concern away and focuses on me. "Well, then. Let's take you to your cousin's house."

We follow her closely, watching the children play in the street. Curious faces observe Yves until we're out of their sight.

Simonne answers Yvonne's knock, her pregnant form blossoming, filling the entrance. Her eyes narrow as they fall on me. "You. What are you doing back?" Before I can answer, her scrutinizing gaze falls on Yves, and she screws up her nose. "And who is this?"

"Simonne. You're looking radiant and as unwelcoming as ever." I smile sweetly, pushing into the house, nudging her aside, and beckon Yves to follow.

"Don't wait to be invited in, will you." She sneers.

"Why would I when I know you would have to invite me in eventually, whether you like it or not." A chuckle stops short on my lips. I can't believe my sweethearted cousin married someone like her. It must be the lack of choice in the village and the pressure to marry into this group if they want to remain accepted in the village.

"Where's Andre?" I ask. Familiar laughter flows into the house from the backyard. "Clearly, he's out back."

We wander through the house and out the back door, spotting Andre sprawled in the sunshine, his parents sitting on either side of him. Simonne's parents face them, their backs toward the house.

Andre spots me. "Ava, you've returned." Careening past his parents-in-law, he lowers to my height to embrace me, and I melt into his chest, trying to push aside all the mixed emotions running through my head.

Gustave and Marie swivel in their seats, their faces expressionless. I ponder for a moment if that's good or not only to have my question pushed aside when I spot Theodore's and Rosa's horrified faces. I struggle to understand their expressions until I realize they're looking at Yves.

Transfixed, a pale-faced Yves mutters, "It's him. It's him. He's the one." He shakes a gnarly finger at Andre, his eyes fearful.

The emotions have been running riot through my body ever since I saw his young face in Yves's memory. Yet I'm determined to weigh all the facts before accusing him. Andre welcomed me from the start, probably exactly as he did Yves when he was a child.

Releasing Andre, I grab Yves's extended hand and squeeze it, whispering into his ear, "It's okay. We'll sort this out. I've got your back with Archangel Gabriel as a backup. I know it's him. I saw him in your memory, remember? I met him last time I was here, so relax. I'll get to the bottom of this."

Fear lurks in Yves's eyes when they flick from Andre to me several times until, eventually, he nods shakily. His hand drops from mine in an act of defeat. I repossess it and lead him forward, observing Andre's confused face.

"What's this lunatic on about?" Theodore demands, standing.

The harshness in his voice takes me aback. He wasn't the friendliest when I met him, but he wasn't aggressive and harsh either. I think about what I saw in Yves's memory, trying to remember if Theodore was also there as a much younger man. His reaction is similar to a guilty man's.

Theodore points at Yves, pulling me from my thoughts. "Why is he acting so weird and pointing at Andre saying, 'It's him, it's him'?" He exaggerates the words, his eyes never leaving Yves, studying him from head to toe.

Gustave stands next to Theodore. "Where did you find this one, Ava? You've outdone yourself this time." He takes a breath to say something else then stops, holding his nose. "He even stinks like he hasn't showered in years."

I glare at Gustave then Theodore. I want to hit them with something—whether it be witch's power, a fist, or a plume of dragon fire, I don't care. I long to inflict harm. Their rudeness to Yves is fuel enough, adding to the thoughts of what Andre may have done to my parents. Although, looking at my cousin's confused face, I'm starting to wonder if he knows. The way Gustave treated me when I met him combined with Theodore's current actions makes me consider whether the finger-pointing was aimed at the wrong person.

Clasping Yves's hand tightly, I lead him farther forward. "Do you recognize him, Uncle?"

Theodore glares at me, horrified. "Why would I recognize this derelict? I don't associate with such kind."

I mimic exaggerated shock. "But he's also a shape-shifter. A crow, to be exact. You should be related, don't you think?"

Theodore places his hands on his hips. "His ability to shift into a bird means nothing. Our shapes don't make us relatives."

Andre looks embarrassed. "Father. Really?"

I glare at Theodore. "Well, this is my new friend. I'm sure I treat him better than someone in this village treated him many years ago."

Gustave stares at Theodore, a shocked expression on his face. "Were you friends with this weirdo?"

My uncle's mouth drops open before sealing with a sneer. "As if I would be friends with someone who looks like that."

"You're much older than my father, aren't you?" I ask.

He looks at me and glares. "What's that got to do with anything?"

I ignore his question and continue. "When my father left the village to move to a cottage that no one could find, you would've had a young child, almost a teen, wouldn't you?"

"And?" His eyes narrow. "I still don't know what that has to do with anything."

I glare back. "Does the name Yves ring a bell?"

He frowns. "No. Why should it?"

I cock an eyebrow. Even though my uncle said no, I'm picking up a lie. Something about his face says he's not telling the truth. Perhaps it's the faint recognition that crosses his face when he looks at Yves.

A small gasp escapes Andre. "Yves?" My cousin squints and approaches him. "Is that really you?"

Yves nods, his face deathly white.

"I wondered where you'd gone." He grabs the older man's hand.

"Andre. Drop it!" Theodore demands.

Andre places his other hand on the back of Yves's gnarled hand. "I hope you're all right, my friend."

Wide-eyed and speechless, Yves nods.

Gustave returns to his seat next to Marie. Their faces remain blank, watching the spectacle unfold.

Ignoring them, I continue with my uncle's interrogation. "Are you sure you don't know him? Because Andre seems to, and your expression tells me otherwise."

"What's that supposed to mean?" The scowl on my uncle's face intensifies.

"This here is Yves. He befriended Andre a little under twenty years ago. He gave Andre my father's location, trusting him with that and not thinking anything of it."

I hear a gasp beside me. Andre drops Yves's hands. "Ava. What are you—"

"Don't speak such rubbish," Theodore interrupts Andre. "I have absolutely no idea who this derelict is. You can't blame me for something my son did. If he asked all the questions, why aren't you asking him? I didn't give away your parents' location. I had nothing to do with your parents' murder." He crosses his arms over his chest.

"What about knowing this man?" I ask.

Theodore squints harder at Yves. "No. I don't know him."

"I'm on the verge of calling you a liar," I accuse him. "Andre would have entrusted you with the information. He was your son, not even a teenager. Besides, I've seen evidence that puts you at my father's house."

"Rubbish! There's no way you've seen evidence that would say otherwise unless you're a witch."

I cock an eyebrow at him. "Is that an accusation or a statement? Tell the truth and stop trying to redirect blame."

"It's an accusation. Seize her!" Theodore yells.

From behind, hands clasp my wrists tightly together, securing me.

CHAPTER TWENTY-SEVEN

"Papa!" Andre cries. "What're you doing?"

My uncle glares at his son. "It's the way of life. Anybody who accuses me of being a traitor or of doing something bad, I can accuse of being a witch."

Andre throws his hands out to the sides. "But she didn't accuse you of doing bad. She just asked if you knew this man." The words blurt out of his mouth.

I wriggle within the grasp, impressed at Simonne's firm hold—she's not weak in her final stages of pregnancy.

"Her mother was a witch, son," my uncle snarls. "Her father was my brother, and he was a shape-shifter, but her mother was a witch. I think I have a pretty good chance of being right."

"But, Papa, what about letting people prove themselves before accusing them?"

"She didn't let me defend myself, and she accused me of something."

"It was merely of knowing this man. Other than his appearance, what's so bad about that? You're acting the opposite of how you taught me to behave."

Andre looks distraught, and I use my most calming voice. "Don't worry, cousin. I've got this."

Uncle Theodore glares at me accusatorially. "Do you? What? Are you going to change into a witch and curse us all?"

I gaze at him in disbelief. "You do remember I shape-shift into a wolf, don't you? I'm pretty sure a wolf can beat a fox and a couple of birds. You don't need witching powers for that."

"If you change into a wolf, then I'll take that as a sign of defiance—another form of attack. I'll call other people from the village to come and help. There are other shape-shifters in this village more powerful than a wolf who will gladly stand by my side." He glances at Gustave and Marie.

I shrug. "I don't need to turn into a wolf." I flick my arms, spinning and breaking Simonne's hold, executing the martial arts training Zacharias taught me over the many years he acted as my guardian. Zacharias taught me how to fight with or without my powers. He is a perfect warrior, always training for the worst case. I remain close to Simonne, my arms crossed while glaring at my uncle. "Is breaking free from your daughter-in-law's restraint classed as a dangerous or hostile act?"

His eyes widen momentarily. He shakes his head slightly, his mouth remaining tight.

"Good. Now, can we talk about this like adults? I'm not accusing you of anything except for knowing this man at one stage in your life. That isn't a crime. I'm trying to get to the bottom of my parents' murder. That's it, and if you have nothing to do with it, then you have nothing to worry about."

"I didn't do it," he snaps.

I huff. He's really trying my patience. "Like I said, I haven't accused you of murdering my parents. I'm merely following the trail to lead me to an answer."

"You better not be a witch." His eyes narrow at me before he glances at Simonne's parents again. Gustave and Marie look surprisingly relaxed and disinterested in the conversation. For a moment, it puts me off. They're acting the opposite of how I thought they would react to the conversation.

Using all my patience, I keep my voice steady, slowly returning my gaze to my uncle. "And what if I am? I'm not binding you, cursing you, or persecuting you. I'm merely standing here, asking questions. It shouldn't matter what form I take. Besides, the witches held me hostage. If I were a witch, why would they do that?"

Simonne's face remains displeased over my easy escape. Her eyes narrow. "It's simple. Because they're witches. They're cruel beings that enjoy persecuting people and shape-shifters, even their own kind."

I roll my eyes and focus on my uncle. "Again, all I want to know is if you know this man."

Theodore intently stares at Yves before approaching

him, stopping a few feet away. His eyes narrow as he studies his features. After a long, silent moment, he nods. "Yes. I believe it's the same man, the one who came to visit Andre when he was ten. He was young. He didn't know any better than to hang around derelicts."

"Papa!" Andre's voice is full of shock and shame. "He's a person."

Slowly I release my breath, trying to keep my sigh of relief silent. Finally, I have an answer. I want to ask my uncle if he used Andre to betray his brother on purpose or if he manipulated Andre to retrieve information from Yves and frame his son for the betrayal. In some ways, it wouldn't surprise me if he did use Andre for betrayal. In other ways, I don't know if he's the conspirator or not. My father was his brother, and he would have to be callous to betray his brother—despite his beliefs.

After his confession, Uncle Theodore removes his gaze from Yves and quickly returns to the seat near his wife.

Instantly, my thoughts turn to Rosa. Her plump face remains emotionless as she observes the scene before her. I think I see a glimpse of bitterness in her eyes as they move from my uncle to Yves then back to Theodore. I can't tell if her bitterness is aimed toward Yves or Theodore for using their son to get to someone else. I would think, after being married to him for so long, she would have a better idea of what he's capable of, unless he's extremely good at hiding the truth.

I push the thought aside. That's up to them to sort

out. "At least you've finally cleared that up. There was no need for theatrics." I stroke my chin. "Although, how come you didn't get Andre to tell Yves he was my father's nephew and that he was passing the information on to you?"

"Why should he? I mean, look at him." He indicates Yves. "Who would befriend him?"

I gaze at him under a raised eyebrow. "Are you saying that Andre was never Yves's friend, that Andre was using him from the start?"

"What?" Andre cries, looking earnestly at Yves. "It's not true. I—"

Theodore cuts him off. "It's not using someone if that's all they're good for. He's only good for one thing. Andre was doing him a favor."

My stomach churns with displeasure. "I can't believe we're related."

Uncle Theodore's mouth turns up into a snarl. "Your father was much the same as me until he met that stupid witch. I've no idea how she got through to him. She must've given him a potion or bewitched him into liking her."

"Pfft! Why would she do that?" I tilt my head.

"Probably just to use him."

"For what?" I ask.

"She probably wanted to see what kind of witch-child she could make when mixed with a shape-shifter."

His rudeness slaps me across the face, and I lean back. "That's just wrong. There're so many good people out there. Witch, shape-shifter, human—it doesn't matter. You should never treat anyone like that, no matter how they look or what their background is. You should treat them by how they act, by what their intentions are—if they're good or bad. That's the way to make loyal friends, not some false loyalty through some pack or village that you live in." I toss my hands out to the sides. "A village that only loves you if you stick to their rules."

He shrugs, as though I hadn't insulted him or the village. "I didn't betray your father. I only told one person that my son had heard from a weirdo where my brother lived."

"Who was that?" I ask.

A sneer creeps on his face. "That was my father. Your grandfather. He was ranting and raving about his youngest son being a coward and running away without facing the music. He was embarrassed over his son turning his back on shape-shifters and marrying a witch, the kind that would persecute shape-shifters and humans, including your grandfather, who narrowly escaped with his life." Theodore stands and paces. "He was beaten to a pulp and tortured. He was lucky he didn't end up maimed. I guess that's the only reason I let Andre continue to meet Yves. Yves looked as though he might have been persecuted by witches and the witches may have deformed him because he was a shape-shifter. But the more I watched Andre hang around him, the more I thought it was just him. That was his 'normal.'"

Yves's eyes fill with sadness, as though he's still feeling the betrayal, and his gaze falls on Andre, the one he thought to be his friend, even though it has been years. One who relayed the information that Yves gave him, passing it on to Theodore, who led other people to his true friends—my father and mother. The pain looks so deep that it distracts him from telling Theodore the truth.

Andre shakes his head, his face horrified. "I di—"

Theodore cuts him off again. "I told my father because he wanted to confront his son. He visited them and told them they needed to separate and that Maurice needed to come back and find a true wife." He stops pacing and narrows his eyes at me. "He told Maurice that he needed to terminate the abomination that he'd created with his witch wife. He didn't want a half witch as a granddaughter."

A furnace of bitterness and rejection burns in my heart, but I keep my face emotionless. I can't believe everything my uncle said. I can see he's a bitter man, willing to say things to hurt people. I saw Andre as a young boy and how he spoke to Yves. It was kind and understanding. It wasn't as Theodore said.

Andre must have gotten his compassion from somewhere. If it was from his father, then something had changed over the years. Either that or Theodore couldn't be bothered with pretending to be nice anymore.

I'm not sure, but I cling to the hope that Andre's

affection stems from his father as a younger man. "And where is my grandfather now?"

Theodore flicks his hand. "He's dead, of course. He would be way too old to have lived this long. Every day, to his deathbed, he blamed me for Maurice's death. He blamed me for being openminded as a child and convincing Maurice it was okay to intermingle with witches." He huffs, repeating his earlier statement. "Yet he was the one who dragged people to my brother's house with his wife and tried to force them to split up. Can you believe the nerve of him?"

I stare at my uncle, confused over the change in tone. Either he's innocent, or he's an excellent liar. I need more time to work out which.

CHAPTER TWENTY-EIGHT

My uncle's face turns hard. "It's probably the witches that killed them anyway, though it should've been a shape-shifter, as punishment for their betrayal."

I blink, dumbfounded. It's almost like he did an about-face in his point of view or his real side is coming out. He's acting like he has a split personality.

"How dare my brother betray us and marry one of the shape-shifter killers. There were so many women in this village he could have married."

Instinctively, I gaze at Andre and his wife, then back to Uncle Theodore. Sarcasm oozes from my voice. "Yeah. Like Andre and Simonne are such a great match. Their shape-shifting forms are completely different, and their ideals and beliefs clash. They can't seem to agree on anything." I lean to one side, cocking a hip and placing my hand on it. "And it wasn't the witches. They would have admitted it proudly. Instead, they denied their involvement but wished they'd had the chance. From what I witnessed in my short time with them—ungraciously chained to a post—I believe they were telling the truth."

At present, my uncle doesn't seem like he would hide it if he were the cause of his brother's death. He seems to despise his brother and everything that he stood for. But this contradiction to the more placid stance not long before confuses me. I long to get to the bottom of it and find out if he knows the truth of my parents' murder.

It takes all my effort to refrain from placing my palm on his forehead and reading his memory, as I did with Yves. This newfound gift is going to burn a hole in my hand. I'm going to want to use it all the time in situations like this. But I know I should follow Archangel Gabriel's advice, and it would be difficult to explain how a shape-shifter has the gift to read minds. It would be confirmation that I'm a witch.

Gustave's and Marie's faces are hard to read. Gustave rubs the balding spot on his head and leans back on his seat. Marie gazes off to the fields, her legs crossed and her head resting on her hand. They've been so quiet during our interaction, adding to my confusion.

Feeling Yves's eyes on me, I glance at him, and he shrugs. I'm dying to take him aside to reread his memory. I need to relook at the faces of the people who visited my parents at the farm. It'll have to wait.

Chewing my nail, I study the shape-shifting crow, trying to remember everything I saw in his mind.

Something moves, distracting me from my study of Yves. Uncle Theodore stands, brushing himself off as though fixing his clothes after a fight. "Well, son. It's time for us to go. We're not staying in this company."

A glance at my aunt, and she stands, ready to follow.

"Why don't you stay longer, Papa?"

I would leave instead if it could wipe that torn expression from Andre's kind face, but the damage is done.

My uncle shakes his head, glancing at Yves, then me. "For as long as you keep company like this, I won't be around. You need to develop better judgment of your acquaintances. Keeping friends like these isn't going to do you any good in this village." Theodore leaves with Rosa following, not once glancing back to give his son reassurance.

The debacle leaves me with a strange kind of happiness. For the first time, I'm glad that I wasn't raised in this village. I'm glad that Piers took me instead of returning me to one of my relatives. Pop must've known. He must've known that this would be how the village would treat me, if they didn't eliminate me.

"Excellent work, Andre." Sarcasm laces Simonne's voice. "You've wrecked a perfectly good day."

As though doused with a bucket of cold water, Andre's face turns hard as he glares at his wife. "How dare you say that to me? How dare you grab Ava like a prisoner and restrain her arms? She's our guest."

My heart swells with his acceptance. Still, I place a hand on Andre's forearm. "It's okay. I can stick up for myself. This is your home, your village. Don't ruin it. You have a baby and your future to consider."

He places his hand on mine, and he looks at me softly. He opens his mouth to speak, only to be interrupted by his wife.

"Don't worry. He already ruined his life," she hisses. "You're just adding to it. I now know where his loyalties lie, and I will never forget this." With a glance at her parents, she waddles into the house, slamming several doors inside the cottage. The last slam leaves me wondering if she left the cottage entirely.

Gustave slaps Andre on the back, and by Andre's reaction, it's harder than a friendly pat. "We're off. Simonne needs our support."

Andre nods and watches as Marie follows Gustave through the cottage. Their faces show no emotion.

Andre sits at the table, propping his cheeks in his hands, and gazes down, shaking his head. I sit opposite him, and Yves joins us, sitting at the end, looking awkward.

"It's not your fault, cousin. I'm sorry this happened. I never meant to bring you turmoil. I was merely trying to find out what happened to my parents and my distant family. I hoped my family would welcome me with open arms."

Andre drags his eyes up to mine, and my heart

breaks over the wells of sadness captured there. "I'm so sorry, Ava. What you've received is far from your hopes. You have a good heart and deserve a better welcome and to be loved." He rests his hand on the table. "After getting to know you, I honestly don't care if you are half witch."

My mouth drops. "Are you sure? Because everybody in this village seems to care."

"What difference does it make? If someone has a good heart, who cares what they look like or where they came from. Shouldn't we all care for each other? Life is hard enough without arguing, fighting, and killing." He shakes his head. "I don't want to raise a baby in a world like this, in a place where people hate and kill over slight differences." He looks mournfully at the cottage door. "I can't believe the way my father acted this afternoon. I hope he and Grandpa didn't have something to do with your parents' deaths. As for Gustave and Marie, they've always hated witches and have been very vocal about it. Their silence was disconcerting." He shakes his head, slamming his forehead onto his hands. "Why are they all so hateful?"

Gently, I rub his forearm. "People fear what they don't understand. I admit I understand these kinds of actions after knowing that these witches have persecuted so many shape-shifters. I've seen firsthand that the witches are not nice people. They didn't give me a chance. They didn't even care if I was part witch. They were too busy accusing me of being a shape-shifter, yet I hadn't even said anything to them about being a shape-shifter. Believe it or not, I had a better reception here, even though people suspect I'm part witch. But one thing I did notice about the witches is that they're not afraid to tell the truth about persecuting someone. I honestly don't believe it was them. I'm holding on to the hope that it wasn't anybody in this village, but I don't know. It's not looking good right now."

Andre straightens, as though something hit him. He picks up a jug then pours Yves and me cups of wine. He grabs plates and starts dishing up some of the leftover food. "I'm sorry. You must be so hungry. I completely forgot that you just arrived after a long trip. I'm such a bad host."

My stomach growls loudly. "You're not a bad host, just slightly distracted." It growls again, and I chuckle. "But I am starving."

Andre hands Yves a plate of food. "I'm so sorry, Yves. I didn't mean to betray your trust when I was younger. I remember Papa asking me questions about you and what you said, but at the age of ten, I didn't think anything of it. I asked you questions he asked me. Then Papa would ask me after I saw you what your answers were." Andre's hands dropped to the table. "I hope I wasn't the reason for their deaths."

Yves's tic sets in before he nods. "Your actions did hurt me many years ago, but today I see that it's not entirely your fault. Because of what your father did, I feel mostly to blame for Ava's parents' demise. I gave you the information you then passed to your father, and I've lived with the guilt for years."

Andre looks genuinely concerned. "I'm so sorry. That was a huge betrayal. I thought my papa was better than that, but unfortunately, he's starting to prove me wrong."

I devour a mouthful of food, savoring the freshly baked bread and roasted meats tantalizing my taste buds. I groan with satisfaction. "This is delicious."

"Yes. My wife is a good cook." Andre's shoulders slump.

CHAPTER TWENTY-NINE

After a tense afternoon, we make our way inside, and I lie awake in my makeshift bed in the corner of my cousin's house. I can't believe that Simonne made Yves sleep outside under the claim of no room in the house. After the cold reception he received earlier, I'm sure he's relieved to stay outside, away from the tension. Still, sleep doesn't come easy for me knowing he's out there alone in a shape-shifter village.

I push the thought from my mind and remind myself that Yves is used to sleeping as a crow out in the elements alongside other wild animals. It saddens me to think of the life he's led—alone for so many years, living outdoors in the elements, facing every storm or blizzard and every scorching day.

Yves indicated it wasn't a big deal. He went without arguing when Simonne kicked him out. Still, I feel terrible that he isn't welcome. There is not much I can do. Simonne barely let me in the house.

Recollections of the afternoon's confrontation play in my mind. I'm surprised how hostile Andre's parents were and confused over the seeming indifference of Simonne's parents. It impressed on me that I need to keep a close eye on all four parents. There must be some way I can extract the truth from them or uncover information that will lead me to the murderer or murderers.

My determination tempts me to use the art of reading minds. I know Archangel Gabriel said I shouldn't do it without the person's permission, yet it would undoubtedly speed up the process of finding out who killed my parents. The only problem is that the shape-shifters wouldn't let me anywhere near them to commit a magical act unless I pinned them down with my powers. That isn't how I want to interact with them.

I wonder if it would work if I did it while they were sleeping. Surely angels don't ask people before they read everyone's minds. Not that I'm putting myself in the class of angels, but I'm desperate to find out the truth, and I can't imagine them allowing me to read their minds if I ask them. I can imagine the stake they would burn me on.

A whirlwind of thoughts fills my head, tossing to and fro whether it's a good idea. I would have to do it in a way that they wouldn't find out, like when they're asleep. Besides, if the person doesn't know, it won't hurt, will it?

The house is silent, and I move to crawl out of bed. Suddenly, someone enters the room. I freeze. My eyes dart to Simonne's pregnant silhouette as light shines from the kitchen, accompanied by the sounds of the preparation of food. Utensils, plates, and pans clang as she prepares her late-night snack. She doesn't try to be quiet. It almost seems as though she's purposefully being noisy, as though my need for sleep means nothing to her. A wave of pity for Andre courses through me— the things he must put up with as her husband. I wonder if there was any kind of love in their marriage at some point in time. Maybe their marriage was arranged by their parents. It wouldn't surprise me if they tried to marry him into a stronger family to make his heir more likely to have a stronger shape-shifting form than a bluebird.

A flash of them smooching when I first met them comes to mind, and I shake my head. There seemed to be love there earlier. Perhaps I'm the turmoil that's been added to their peace.

Hiding my face, I watch Simonne prepare her little midnight snack then return to her room. I wait for quite some time after, until I think I hear her heavy breathing again. Uttering a spell, I turn invisible and tiptoe to the entrance of their room. I push at the slightly ajar door. Simonne's back faces the entrance. Slipping through the small opening, I stand in front of her, waiting for a reaction. Her chest rises and falls, and her eyes flicker like they're in a dream. It should be safe to go.

Tiptoeing out of the room, I remain in my invisible form and exit the house. I haven't been to her parents' house, but Andre pointed out where they lived one of the times we walked down the street. Lavender lines the pathway, and my anxiety dampens slightly when the scent of the flowers fills my nostrils. Unlocking the door with my witch powers, I quietly push it in. The thrill of doing something I shouldn't fires through my veins. The sound of deep breathing directs me to the open door of their bedroom.

With silent feet, I approach Gustave and hold my hand gently to his forehead. His forehead wrinkles under my palm, as though he's having a bad dream. I pick out sections of his life, rewinding to nearly twenty years ago when he stands there watching his wife holding his baby in her arms, a little girl that is most likely Simonne. Love overflows his heart as he looks at his baby daughter, yet something dark broods in the background. A deep worry clouds his feelings, over-powering the joy that he feels.

I listen as a man with features that remind me of my uncle tells Gustave how Theodore found out where his brother lived—the one that shamed the shape-shifters and married a witch. Spittle comes from the older man's mouth as he exposes that the shambles of a marriage produced a baby—a half shape-shifter and half witch.

Grabbing hold of that memory, I follow it until it leads me to accompany the group of people who visited my parents' farm. Try as I might, I can't find Gustave visiting and murdering them himself, though the hatred in his heart for my father and his interbreeding mani-fests strong and true. Surely if he killed my parents, I would find it as I search his past.

Removing my hand, I stare at Gustave's face a few

moments, watching him breathe deep and slow. His teeth gnash in his sleep, imitating his shifter form of a wild dog. He's a proud father and honored to be part of his race. I admire that part of him. In his head, I also picked up how he doesn't trust me, and he's sure that I'm part witch. Seeing his certainty in my heritage, I wouldn't be surprised if most of the village already suspects what I am. I have to be careful. I can't let my guard down at any time.

The other side of the bed stirs. I pull my eyes from Gustave to watch Marie as she tosses in her sleep. I move around to the other side of the bed and watch her for a few minutes. Her face creases into a frown then relaxes. In the very dim light, she's quite attractive without all the worry.

When her tossing subsides, I kneel beside her and place a hand on her forehead, sifting through her memories. Her distrust for me shines through from the beginning, intensified because I'm associating with Yves. It's a strange feeling, entering someone's head and picturing their true feelings about me. There are no pretenses or niceties. It's one hundred percent raw truth.

I sift back to the day they visited my parents' place. Surprise surfaces when I discover she was also involved. The argument between my father and his village shape-shifters repeats over again. The disappointment and hatred toward my father surface because of his marriage to my mother. These people are a small village with small minds. They need to open their horizons, travel a bit, and meet other people.

Still, who betrayed my parents eludes me as I sift through Marie's memories. Marie leaves at the same time as the rest of them on the day of the argument, and I don't find evidence of her returning. It appears that the group of shape-shifters mainly confront my parents, fearing what it will do to their lives and the lives of their extended family if they remain together. Their actions are based more on the protection of their home and village. They don't want the witches to find their community. After everything the witches have done to their families, they don't want any relation married to a witch. Along with hatred, they feel concern, for their families and their children are their main priorities.

A deep, warm love emerges in me when Marie thinks of her family, and I can understand the shape-shifters' motives even though I feel they're unrealistic. I know I'm not the best person to judge, for I am the child of a witch and a shape-shifter. Naturally, I would be more openminded over my presence than these people.

Removing my hand from her forehead, I stand, remaining in the room for a few more minutes, watching them sleep. It's hard to process what I've seen. I was sure these two would have known who the betrayers or murderers were. I was wrong. Their joy and relief over my parents' deaths are disturbing but not a crime, nor is the fact that they didn't try and find my parents' killers. They were glad they had one less problem to deal with. As for me, it's true that they thought I was dead. The report stated that my parents' place was covered in blood, body parts lying everywhere. It would've been almost impossible to know I was alive. Still, in my eyes, it's a crime that they didn't bury my parents. Coming up empty, I contemplate my next move, trying to decide who should be the next one to investigate. It takes all my concentration to focus on Yves's memory and press through the faces. I recognized a couple more people in the memory. I'm sure of it. Matching the faces to the current owner proves difficult.

As I listen to the low rumble of their snoring, I close my eyes and focus on those faces. The slant of the male's eye feels as though it should be triggering a memory, yet it taunts me, remaining out of reach. Tearing my vision away from him, I focus on the woman. There is a dimple on one cheek that looks strangely familiar. I press my eyes closed more tightly, feeling the creases on the outer corners of my eyes deepen from the pressure. Again, something is telling me I know this woman, yet I just can't grasp who she is.

As silently as I came, I exit the house past the rows of lavender. The purple stems point to the sky, looking eerily enticing in the moonlight, marking the path to the road. The smell of lavender wafts up to my nose, relaxing my muscles as I remain invisible and walk down the street and return to Andre's house.

CHAPTER THIRTY

L oud banging sounds from the kitchen. I stretch my legs over the edge of the makeshift bed and rub the sleep from my eyes. Simonne stomps around the kitchen, preparing breakfast. Her body language is cold and rigid, expressing her displeasure over having unwanted people in her house. I sigh softly. It would be nice if we could get along. I enjoy Andre's company, and it saddens me that his wife doesn't feel the same about me.

Simonne absentmindedly rubs her rounded belly as she prepares things in the kitchen. I wonder what kind of shape-shifter the baby will be—a weak little bluebird or a stronger animal like a fox.

My stomach growls at the thought of food. It was a long night, and I worked up an appetite. Attempting to break the silence with Simonne, I force a cheerful voice. "Would you like some help?"

The muscles in her back tense more, and my shoulders slump. I can't even speak to her without her cringing or turning more rigid.

"There's nothing to help with." She speaks through gritted teeth after a moment's pause. "We're using up bread and leftovers from yesterday."

Sitting up, I shrug. "Well, if there's anything I can do, let me know. I don't want to be a burden."

She shoots daggers with her eyes. "Then you know what to do." Spite riddles her voice. She slams a plate on the table.

I know she wants me to leave, but it's not just her house—it's also Andre's. Although the way things are going, I'll probably leave shortly. First, I need to finish my business.

Simonne nods to a kitchen chair and hisses, "Well? Do you have to wait for an invitation?"

I take my place at the table. "Thank you." Despite what she thinks of me right now, I'm going to make an effort to prove that not all witches are nasty, especially after confirming that her parents didn't betray or murder my parents. Even though they haven't confirmed that I'm a witch, they're on the brink of stating it. As much as I don't appreciate the ill-treatment and I don't deserve it, I still hang on to the hope that I can change her mind.

Dragging my plate toward me, I pick at the contents.

Andre walks into the room. "Morning."

A weight lifts off my shoulders. I'm no longer alone

with the ice queen. "Morning," I say with half a mouthful.

Glancing at his wife's stiff form, he turns to me and smiles. "Did you sleep well?"

I nod, shoving more food into my mouth.

"That's a lie. She was out of her bed again." Simonne's eyes narrow at me, daring me to deny it.

Andre's jaw drops, and he catches the glare Simonne gives me. "Are you spying on her all the time?" A biting nastiness taints his voice.

Simonne points to her belly. "I can't help it if I can't sleep because of the baby. When I can't sleep, I get up and walk around, and every time she stays here, her bed is empty."

"Sorry." I shrug. "I can't help it if I have to use the bathroom."

Andre gestures to me as though my statement explains it all. "See? You're making a big deal out of nothing. It's not unusual for people to go the toilet in the middle of the night."

Simonne slams a plate full of food in front of an empty chair, and Andre sits before it, biting off a chunk of bread.

"Can you not see? Just because she's your cousin doesn't make her a good person. She's half witch, half shape-shifter, an abomination!"

His shoulders slump. "Are we going to do this again?"

He turns to me, and I continue eating. I'm not going

to be part of their argument—not verbally anyway. But clearly, I can't help being the center of it.

He indicates to me. "She's tiny, and she hasn't done anything but be nice since she got here. She's nothing like the witches, witch blood or not."

"It's a facade," Simonne hisses. She pushes her chair back and grabs her plate. "I'm going to eat elsewhere." Angrily, she waddles out the door to the backyard.

Andre drops the bread in his hand onto his plate. "I'm sorry about that."

I pick at a piece of bread. "It's okay. I wish it were different, but it's not. At least I found you. That brings me joy."

His eyes cloud with sadness. "You came here to find your family and to fit in with other people of your kind. You've lost so much. Yet all you've received here is malice. After so long, I can't believe people hold a grudge against you, even people who weren't yet born when your parents were killed. The village taught the legend of your parents to the next generation, and it saddens me."

Looking deep into his eyes, I touch his forearm. "Children only know what their elders teach them. Look at how your father manipulated you when you were ten."

A deeper sadness fills his eyes.

"No. Don't be sad. My point is that you were a young boy. You didn't know any better, and you trusted your father. As for your father, I understand the hatred toward the witches. I really do. I've seen firsthand what they can do, and I was only there for a few hours. I was lucky Yves followed me to help me out."

I slump back into my chair. "But my mother couldn't have been like them. She must've wanted to leave the coven. I can only imagine that when she met my father that gave her the last bit of courage she needed, the final push to leave the coven and start a new life." I run a hand over my head. "It's unfortunate that it led to their deaths. I'm just lucky that they were smart enough to think ahead and send me away with their human friend, one that the murderers knew nothing about. Otherwise, they would have pursued him as well."

He nods. "I simply wish it was different." He takes a sip of his juice, and I bite down on the crusty bread.

Andre's eyes land on the fourth empty chair. "Where's Yves?" His search continues around the room as if looking for him.

"He hasn't come back since Simonne said he wasn't welcome. Although I thought he would come back for breakfast. I'll go out looking for him later. If it's okay, I'll grab some food for him."

"Of course, it is. I'll come with you."

We finish our food quickly, and I wash the dishes while he prepares to depart, leaving Simonne to fume in the backyard.

Immediately after leaving the house, I scan the tree-tops of the village.

Andre searches the closer grounds and the streets of Vezelay. "Where did he say he would be for the night?"

"He didn't mention a spot, but he likes to hang around the forest. That's what he's known most of his life anyway." I point in the distance. "He's probably at the edge of the village looking out from the forest. He tends to do that. We should listen for any calls from a crow."

We fall into silence, taking our time walking the streets and listing to every birdcall of the early morning. Birds chirp happily from the trees nearby, yet not one is the caw of a crow.

As we near the forest, my concern escalates. I study every tree lining the woods. "Have you heard anything?"

Andre shakes his head.

"That's unusual. Typically, he would caw by now. Most of the time, he spots me with his crow eyes well before I have a chance to spot him." I frown. "Hopefully, he's just taken off and is out exploring or perhaps catching breakfast." Anxiously, I fiddle with the little package I hold in my hand containing his food.

We hit the edge of the forest, and I search the trees. Even though crows are black, they're not easy to see among the dense leaves. I call, "Yves!"

Silence is my answer. Even the wildlife falls quiet.

I press forward and call again, "Yves!"

Andre joins me. "Yves!"

Worrying my lip, I scan the treetops and lower branches. "He shouldn't have gone much farther in.

The only reason he's staying is to accompany me. He's got to be around here somewhere."

We wander in farther and circle the edge of the forest surrounding the village while continuing to call. Not a sound comes from a crow. A knot forms in my belly, the tension making me sick.

I rub my creased forehead. "I don't like this. It's unusual for him to disappear. Even if he was hunting, he wouldn't go far, and he would answer me."

The worry creases gather around Andre's eyes. We press deeper into the forest.

I call again, "Yves!"

A strange sound reaches me. It's almost like a groan.

I spin around and follow the noise, my eyes darting everywhere as I search the ground. "Yves!" I hear it again, and from the corner of my eye, I see movement. I pivot and look in that direction. A bare foot sticks out from behind a tree, and I run, hearing Andre's footsteps not far behind me. My heart pounds in my ears, blocking out any further sounds.

More leg appears from behind the trunk, hairy and naked. I dart around the side of the tree and spot an unclothed Yves, his face bloodied and his arm hanging in a weird position. The expression on his face is distant, and his are eyes closed.

Yanking the backpack off my back, I pull out a cloth and throw it over his lower half. Bruises cover most of his body, and I'm shocked at some of the locations I find them as I observe his semiconscious form. Studying his leg, I notice his foot angled in an awkward position.

Blood mattes his gray hair and beard. His eyes are swollen and bruised.

"Oh, Yves! What happened to you?" Searching for answers, my eyes connect with Andre's, reading all kinds of fear and apprehension there.

CHAPTER THIRTY-ONE

I touch his skin. He's freezing. "We have to get you back to the house." I glance up at my cousin, and he nods.

Andre squats and laces his arm underneath Yves's armpits, throwing the crow shape-shifter's arm over his shoulder. He pushes up, taking most of the weight, leaving me scurrying around the other side to do the same. I wrap the fabric around Yves's waist and tie it into a knot, securing it in place. He appears slightly more alert after the movement. Using one leg, he helps us move him toward the cottage.

"What happened to you, Yves? Did someone do this to you?" My stomach churns with the thought of him being a victim of someone's abuse.

He answers with a slow, broken groan. His neck is swollen and bruised, causing me to think he may have some damage to his voice box. I hope this isn't the case. I need to find out how this happened.

Our progress is slow, burdened with his full weight each time he takes the pressure off his good foot. His groans of pain are minimal, even though I can tell every part of him hurts. Our attempt to move him causes him an extreme amount of pain. Trying to ease this, I move my grasp to his arm, careful to avoid his wrists and the broken bone.

"Wait!" I cry, struggling under his weight. "This isn't going to work. We're hurting him too much. His ankle's broken, and so is his arm. I need to shift, and you need to throw him on my back."

Andre stares at me blankly, blinking slowly. "But you're a wolf. Wolves are big, but they can't carry a man on their back."

I expel a deep breath. "Yes, I am a wolf—among other things."

He frowns. "What's that supposed to mean?"

"Look. Don't panic. It's still me, okay?" Without waiting for an answer, I shift into a horse.

Andre gawks, his feet fixed to the spot. The few minutes seem like hours as I wait for the shock to pass. I flutter my meaty lips, and suddenly, he sparks into action and throws the older man facedown over my back. It's not the most comfortable for Yves, but he won't have to travel far. Andre walks beside me, securing Yves on my back as I move quickly and smoothly.

I can feel his eyes studying my haunches and body as we walk. My hooves clip-clop on the stone street until we stop outside Andre's cottage. Andre grabs Yves off my back, taking his time to be careful, trying to cause Yves as little pain as possible. When he reaches his doorway, he gives me a last glance. I gallop into the forest and shift to my human form. I grab my bag from where I left it behind a tree, throw on my clothes, and walk back to the village. My intention wasn't to spook my cousin, but I had to do something to help Yves. I have so many gifts, and I hate to watch a friend in pain just to keep them a secret.

Entering Andre's home quietly, I spot Yves on my makeshift bed. Andre crouches over him, tending to his wounds the best he can.

"Here. Let me help." I grab the washcloth from him and wash Yves's wounds.

Working on one limb at a time, I straighten his breaks. His screams of pain pierce my ears before I drown in his moans of agony as I strap his straightened limbs, bracing them in splints.

Andre cringes with each scream, yet he doesn't pull his gaze from the injured man as Yves goes through the realigning process. There's a strange tension in the air, and I can tell he wants to ask me questions but holds off. He glances at my dwindling bandage supply and leaves Yves's side momentarily, then returns with more wraps.

After everything is set correctly, I dig through my bag until my fingers brush a smooth surface. I extract the small bottle, uncork the lid, and sniff the murky contents. The smell of rosemary, lavender, and chamomile waft up, the pleasant part of the bottle's contents. Before I left my farm, I grabbed several useful potions I'd mixed prior, ones that could be beneficial on my trip.

I tilt the opening to Yves's lips. "Drink."

Andre eyes the bottle. "What's that?"

"It's a little medicine I picked up. I always like to bring it with me when I travel, in case I get hurt somehow and I'm on my own. It helps the body heal faster."

Yves's trusting eyes study me as he drinks slowly, almost a drop at a time. I don't know if Andre suspects it's a potion. If he does, he doesn't say anything. Instead, he squats by the older man's side and holds his head steady so I can pour the liquid without spilling.

Simonne enters and scoffs, giving us a nasty glare. "I can't believe you two." She shakes her head before stomping back out the door. I briefly watch her retreat.

Andre's eyes follow his wife. "Don't worry about her. She has to get over her grudge against people who aren't one hundred percent shape-shifters."

When my precious potion bottle is empty, Andre lowers Yves's head to the pillow before he enters the kitchen to make us a cup of tea.

"How long will the medicine take to work?"

I plunk down on a chair, exhaustion seeping into my body. "It should work fairly quickly. I don't usually need the whole bottle, but Yves's injuries were significant."

He nods once, his eyes never leaving me as he places a cup of tea in front of me. The silence is awkward, and so is his constant observation of me. Finally, he breaks the silence, keeping his voice low. "So, are you going to tell me the whole story?"

In a half tease, I lower my voice to the same level as his and ask, "Is that the story of how I can change into more than one shape?"

He nods.

"That's pretty much the story. I can change into many different shapes, not just one, almost any form I want to take on. I've had the gift from birth. I didn't know that the shape was supposed to be restricted to one until I arrived here. I don't know why I have this gift when others don't. I thought it was a natural thing for shape-shifters."

I twiddle my thumbs on my lap, glancing down at them briefly before returning my gaze to Andre. "Do you think any differently of me?" I study his expression, searching for any evidence of a lie. "The only reason I didn't tell you was because I didn't want to shock or overload you with a new possibility when your people live with such closed minds. I tossed all of that aside when I saw Yves in so much pain. I knew we had to get a better mode of transport, so I changed in front of you. Whatever the risk, I couldn't let my friend suffer like that."

After studying me a moment more, Andre shakes his head. "No. You're still the same person. I don't believe that makes any difference. You just happen to have more cool shapes to turn into. It would probably make a lot of the shape-shifters jealous." His eyes don't leave me, and another awkward silence falls over us. Eventually, he asks, "Are you a witch also?"

I swallow the lump in my throat. I long to keep his friendship. His admission yesterday afternoon after the big family argument in the backyard comes to memory. He said he didn't care anymore if I was a witch or not. I trust my instincts and cling to the hope that he meant it. He showed me kindness even though the majority of the shape-shifters in his village wrote me off.

My eyes meet his, and I hold his gaze before moving my head up and down a couple of times. Lowering my voice to a whisper, trying to stay out of Simonne's earshot, I say, "I understand if you want me to move out of your house to protect your family. This village could be quite savage if they found out."

"Yes. You're right. This village is quite savage when it comes to witches, but I'm not going to turn you out—despite what my wife thinks. I'm certain you're a good person and you won't use your witching powers against us."

"I can't guarantee that for everyone. I will use it against someone if I have to, especially if someone I love is in danger."

He nods. "I can understand that. Can you heal?"

I shake my head. "No. The best I can do is potions, which I've already given Yves." I toss him a cheeky expression. "Which I'm sure you already assumed."

He smirks. "So, I guess we just have to wait."

Yves groans, and I dart to his side to hold his uninjured hand.

"I'm here, Yves. I'm here. You're safe now."

His eyes slit open, and he lightly squeezes my hand. When his mouth moves, I put my ear close. A sound escapes his throat as undefined words. He appears to be having trouble speaking. I move my ear within an inch of his mouth. I don't want to ask him to repeat something when I know it hurts him to speak. Yves releases my hand and holds his hand to his throat. "A hawk."

I pull back and frown at him. "Did you just say a hawk?"

He nods slightly.

"Did a hawk attack you?"

He holds up two fingers.

My eyes widen. "Two hawks attacked you?"

He nods once before resting his head on the pillow. His eyes close, and a raspy snore escapes his mouth.

CHAPTER THIRTY-TWO

The blood drains from my face, and my cheeks turn clammy. Two hawks. Two hawks attacked Yves. I don't want to think about it. I really don't. The shifter hawk I know of in the village is my uncle. I pace the floor before turning to Andre. "How many hawks are in this village?"

His face pales as silence once again cuts through the air. His attempt to say something lodges in his voice box. He clears his throat and looks to the ground. "Two. There are two hawks."

My eyes widen. "You don't think…" I pause for a moment. "Do you?" My voice is a whisper, the volume suppressed by horror.

His eyes remain downcast as he shakes his head and shrugs. "I don't know. I hope not… but I don't know."

"Who else besides your father is a hawk here?"

"Henri's father. That's how we were assigned to security, because our fathers were hawks. They're in charge of watching out for the village. The responsibility was automatically passed on to us, even though our shapes are a disappointment to them. We can't do anything as bluebirds other than watch and fly around and bring word back to the hawks. We can't attack anyone."

"Why would they attack Yves? Your dad shunned him and wasn't happy about his presence, but I didn't think he would attack Yves." I pace again. "Do you think it has anything to do with my parents and their murder? And because Yves identified you, which led to your father when we turned up at the house?"

It takes Andre a few moments to answer. He shuffles his feet. "I would like to think my father's innocent, but that would be natural to think of your own family. I would hope Henri's father would be the same."

I nod, expressing my understanding. "I thought his parents would be of good character. Do you think Henri's father was one of the men who turned up at my parents' house—one of the people we haven't identified yet?"

He shakes his head as though ridding it of the thought. "Surely, it can't be him. He was nice to you. I... I don't know. It pains me to say that not too many people here have been pleasant to you or Yves. It could be any one of those who weren't. Maybe it was Simonne's parents. A healthy hate of witches has been embedded in her from her upbringing."

It pains me, but I answer with the truth. "No. It's not them."

"How do you know?" He brings his cup of tea to his lips.

"Because I visited them last night when they were sleeping, and I read their minds."

He splutters his drink back into the cup. "You what?" He thumps his chest, trying to clear the tea that went the wrong way. His hand covers his nose and mouth.

I release a pent-up breath and repeat, "I read their minds. I looked into their past and saw their actions."

He lowers the cup of tea, his hand shaking slightly. "I've never heard of that before."

"It's a new gift I just received or, rather, was taught."

"By whom? I haven't heard of witches being able to do that." He crosses his legs and brings the cup to his lips again.

"It wasn't a witch who taught me."

"It can't be a shape-shifter." He looks certain of his statement.

"No. It was an archangel."

The cup shatters on the floor, spilling the hot drink. "A what?"

Squatting, I pick up the broken pottery pieces. "An archangel. I have friends who are archangels. I was also raised by an archangel when my guardians were killed."

He remains fixed to his chair as though stuck. "You've lived an interesting life, haven't you?" He eyes me from under a raised eyebrow. "There's nothing orthodox about you. How did you convince an archangel to become your guardian?"

"I didn't convince him. He came to me." I throw the broken pieces in the trash and pick up a towel. "He was ordered to protect me for some reason, and he came and lived with me before my guardian parents were killed. My guardian archangel raised me like a daughter, living with me and watching over me until I was old enough to look after myself. He helped me meet Jehan, my husband." I wring my hands. "But he was also killed." Tears well in the corners of my eyes, and I push them back.

Sympathy leaks from every pore in Andre's body. "Where was your archangel when this happened?"

Sitting down, I scrunch the material of my skirt in my lap. "Battling demons with me. It was too late when we realized something was wrong. The leader of the archangels took me back to my cabin only to be captured by demons, and Zacharias, my guarding archangel, followed us and freed him only to be rendered earthbound, his wings amputated." I wipe more tears from my face with my sleeve. "He is buried so deep in mourning, tearing himself up for his short-comings and predicament, that he refuses to see me."

Andre holds my trembling hands, stilling them from tearing at my skirt.

Clarity knocks me on the head, and I stand. "Actually, I think it's best if I leave. Everyone I seem to get close to gets murdered."

Andre stands and gently forces me back down with

a hand on my shoulder, taking the cloth from my hands. "Don't be ridiculous. For one, you're not leaving Yves here by himself. And two, I'm not letting you go, whether you think you can look after yourself or not."

I stare deep in his eyes. "I don't want anything to happen to you—or your unborn child. Even though I haven't gotten along with your wife, I don't want anything bad to happen to her either."

He doesn't budge when I try to move past him. "I'm not abandoning you. You came here looking for family, and I want to be that family."

I grasp his hand and squeeze it. "Thank you," I whisper. "I appreciate it, but it sounds like I have to give your father an unpleasant visit. I need to find out who the hawks are."

"I understand. I hope it's not him, just some random hawks from the wild or shape-shifters visiting from another village."

"Me too."

CHAPTER THIRTY-THREE

Territorial protection fuels my devotion to find Yves's attackers and my parents' murderers. The trip to my origins was meant to connect me with family members, bringing me more people to care about. It has done this, yet regrettably, it's turning into a hunt for justice, a mission to obliviate. Shape-shifters and witches have enough enemies without betraying their own. The witches I will work on later. First, I must get to the bottom of my friend's and parents' mistreatment.

With purposeful footsteps, I stomp through the streets of Vezelay. A woman passes me, her path changing to the opposite side of the road. Her movements capture my attention, and our eyes connect. Her mouth pushes into a flat line, emphasizing a dimple in one cheek, tugging the strings of my memory. I study the rest of her features. That's the woman I saw visiting my parents' place in Yves's memory. I frown. There's something else. I've seen her recently. It takes a moment. That's Yvonne's mother.

The woman catches my glare and returns my suspicion. I mark her in my memory. I'll have to look into her further if I don't find what I'm looking for with this visit. I hope for Andre's sake that I prove his father wasn't involved. He has enough to deal with in Simonne.

Traveling down the road, I reassess the quaintness of the village. It isn't as secluded as the cottages I grew up in, but its roads lined with cottages are picturesque and appeal to me more than the village where Jehan's parents reside. It's hard to believe that such a beautiful place can harbor so much hostility, bred deep into the souls of the occupants.

Pebbles scatter behind me. I turn, only to find the street empty. Pausing, I study the street. Unable to find the cause, I continue, the hairs on the back of my neck standing on end. I can't shake the feeling that someone's following me.

Mixed emotions fill me when I reach my uncle's place. He's the brother to my father and the father to my cousin, both of whom I hold dear. It's bittersweet knowing he may be the answer to Yves's attack and possibly my parents' deaths. A rabbit scoots past my legs. I start, holding a hand over my heart as it disappears down the side of the cottage.

I raise my fist, ready to knock, when the door swings open.

My uncle's smiling face appears on the other side.

"Ava. Come in." He stands back, grandly motioning for me to enter. Hesitation grips me down to my soles, and my feet refuse to move. His behavior is different than last time, confusing me all over again. Clasping my wrist, he jerks me inside, the smile remaining fixed on his face. He peers over my shoulder to the street. "Are you here on your own?"

In an attempt to rid my brain of fogginess, I shake my head and clear my throat. "Yes." Not sure what the question meant.

"Lovely. Then come. Rosa will prepare you a lovely cup of tea." He releases my wrist and waves me extravagantly toward the kitchen with an expectant air that I should oblige.

The cloud of uncertainty swamps me as I trek to his dining room. He pulls out a seat and indicates for me to sit, before disappearing. The legs of the chair moan against the floor as I drag it to the back of my knees and sit.

Rosa's plump, soft skin brushes mine as she hurries to the stove top with a pot of water, placing it on the hot plate. She faces me wearing a broad smile. "How nice of you to come to visit." Her eyes flick expectantly to the entrance. "Didn't Andre come with you?"

I shake my head. "I left Andre to take care of a friend." I brush my skirt's material covering my lap, straightening it until it flows to the floor.

"Oh, how nice." Rosa's smile broadens. "We have your company all to ourselves."

"Yes," I say hesitantly, not quite sure what to make

of their strange behavior. They haven't been this nice to me the whole time I've been in town.

"How lovely." Rosa beams. She leans into the cupboard and pulls out a teapot and tea leaves, measuring them into the pot. "And who is this friend Andre's looking after?"

"It's Yves," I say with spite.

"Oh." Rosa's voice is high-pitched, her smile broadens. "Nice." She busies herself more, plunking the pot of sugar and cups on the table.

Every move she makes I watch, unable to shake the feeling that something's off. She didn't react how I expected her to when I mentioned Yves. Instead, she's acting as though she's never heard of him and that her disapproval and disagreement from the other day is nonexistent. Once again, my aunt's and uncle's attitudes are throwing me off. They have gone from being nasty and spiteful to suddenly being nice.

Theodore pulls out a chair opposite me at the kitchen table, in front of a cup Rosa laid out. His movements are sure and confident, lacking any hint of anger or resentment. He shuffles his cup and spoons sugar into it. As though sensing that he's being watched, his eyes flick up and meet mine. A tender smile spreads across his face.

I pull my eyes from him and frown into my cup. I'm not sure what's going on. After everything I've been through, I decide to play along and wait and see. I'm not sure if it was Theodore, wild hawks, or somebody else who attacked Yves.

The water boils, and Rosa hoists the pot to the table, pouring the hot water into the teapot. She places the teapot in the middle as the leaves soak and the tea infuses the water.

Something clatters in the next room, and I spin to have a better look.

Rosa chuckles. "Oh, don't mind that. Is probably my pet rabbit. It's always getting up to mischief."

"I didn't know you had a pet rabbit." I grab my spoon and shovel a teaspoon of sugar into my cup.

Grabbing the teapot, Rosa pours the tea into my cup. "That's probably our fault, dear. We haven't invited you around to get to know you. We've been a little distracted. Forgive us." She clucks. "And right at the time you came and wanted to get to know us." She shakes her head then pours tea into Theodore's cup. "But you're here now, so this is a perfect opportunity to sit down and have a nice cup of tea. Don't you think?"

"Sure." I play along. From my short experience, it seems better to be friendly when I need to retrieve information from people. They seem more obliging. I blow on the hot tea, my mind working overtime. It scalds my lips when I take a tiny sip, and I put the cup down. Sitting back against my seat, I link my hands behind the back of my chair.

Having finished stirring, Uncle Theodore clinks his spoon against the rim of his cup. "I hear that you went to visit the witches."

"Yes. I did."

"I trust you found it helpful." The spoon clatters lightly as he tosses it on the table.

I puff out a dissatisfied breath. "Actually, I found it very unhelpful. They were uncooperative, and all they did was tie me up near a firepit and demand I prove I'm a witch and a shape-shifter."

My uncle leans back against his chair. "Did they not know you're a half witch—that you're Suzanne's daughter?"

"I told them I was her daughter. They didn't care. They still wanted me to prove that I had witching powers."

Uncle Theodore's eyebrow quirks, and I wonder what it means.

"And I'm sure you proved it to them, you know"— he flicks a hand nonchalantly—"to save your soul."

Suddenly, my arms are trapped from behind. I gaze over my shoulder to find Jeanne, the lady I saw on the street earlier. Yvonne's mother ties my hands together with my palms facing each other. I sense a second pair of hands helping and gaze over my other shoulder to find Henri's father.

"What's going on?" I ask, squirming.

My uncle leans forward, his eyes trained on me. "We know you're a witch. Anyone who leaves the witches' coven alive is a witch."

I roll my eyes. "I told you already. Yves saved me. Nothing I did would gain their favor."

Rosa's eyes narrow in on me, a sudden change in

her face. "So, you did prove you're a witch, to save your soul?"

Quickly, I assess the situation. It's no use pretending anymore, trying to stop them from knowing the full truth. It was probably stupid in the first place because they knew I was born from a witch as soon as I said whose daughter I was. In a casual voice, I say, "Yes. I did prove that I have witching powers, but that doesn't make me like them, just as it didn't make my mother like them. I completely agree with you. They are evil, and they do deserve to be treated badly, but that's purely because of how they treat other people—not because of what's in their blood or that they hold witch power." My eyes land on each one of them, including Henri's father and Jeanne. "I'm certain you will feel better in your conscience if you treat me as I've treated you. Surely you know by now that my intentions are good. I haven't raised one hand against any of the shape-shifters in this village."

Theodore rises to his feet and glowers down at me. "That doesn't matter. You have witch blood running through your veins, and that's how you'll treat us eventually. So, we will end this now. You must be killed, just like your father and mother were killed."

Holding my jaw firm, I gaze straight into his eyes. "Did you kill my parents?"

"We did." Pride fills Theodore's voice. "All four of us, plus my father."

"But how? He was a strong shape-shifter, and she was a witch." As heartbreaking as it was, I had to know.

"While they were sleeping, we hit your father hard across his head, rendering him unconscious. Then we tied your mother's hands, much the same as yours." A smirk rises to his face, turning the depths of my stomach. "We then woke your mother. That way she could watch us dismember your father as his consciousness returned, watch as he screamed for mercy. Then we did the same to her." His eyes glide down my arms to my hands secured behind my back. "You witches are useless without your hands."

He paces, letting the filthiness of the information sink in, churning hot anger through my veins. He continues, "It gave me so much pleasure seeing the horror on her face as we cut your father." He pauses. "It was even better when I got to hear the screams of the witch as we finished her off. The only disappointment was that we couldn't find you."

The anger sears through my veins, the heat intensifying, making it impossible to control. It weaves through my veins like hot lava cutting through the rocks of a volcano—destroying everything in its wake. Every cell of my body burns until I can no longer manage it. My body dissipates into particles, reforming into the burning form of a dragon. The cottage presses in on my sides, and the roof pushes up and out, crashing into piles of rubble on the floor around my feet. The slates of the roof smash on the hard ground inside the kitchen.

Fear possesses each face in front of me. Jeanne shape-shifts, shrinking into a hare and charging for an exit. Stooping, I clasp her long ear between my sharp teeth, pulling back and ripping it from her head. The hare squeaks from fear and pain, cowering in the corner. Henri's father changes into a hawk and tries to take to the sky. I clasp him in my talons, squeezing until I hear bones crack. Rosa runs to the door, and I stomp my foot in her path. She backs away with her hands raised in surrender. Theodore transforms into a hawk, and I clamp my teeth down on his wing. He screeches in pain.

The four treacherous people who killed my parents remain in this room, and my anger burns so deep that I'm losing control.

Theodore returns to his human form, his body naked and in pain on the floor, his arm lying in an unnatural position. He stares at me, crying for mercy, "No. Please stop. What are you?"

CHAPTER THIRTY-FOUR

I t occurs to me that their kindness when I arrived was only a ruse to lure me in the door and into the kitchen. They must have thought that if they secured me, tying my hands, rendering my witching powers useless, then my only option would be to turn into a wolf—a force to be reckoned with but something that can still be defeated. Somehow, they thought that the four of them could trap me in the kitchen and finish me off. Two hawks, a rabbit, and I'd heard Rosa was a wild boar. I huff. They were wrong.

Towering over them, I glare down with fiery dragon anger churning in my veins. It's near impossible to refrain from snapping at a chunk of their flesh. With these dangerous emotions coursing through me, my mentality is set to destroy. And how I long to destroy them. I clasp Uncle Theodore within my talons and hold his naked form in the air above the shattered slates barely clinging to the remainder of his roof.

A gasp reaches my dragon ears. I turn to see a woman running down the street in the opposite direction, her wide eyes connecting with mine as she glances over her shoulder. My vengeful eyes land back on my uncle. I long to rip his head off and spit it far away, repeating the process with each of the traitors lying within the room below.

Flashes of my parents' death mixed with the description recently given run through my head, images of how these spineless shifters ambushed them while they were asleep, not giving them a chance. They have no remorse or regret, and now they want to do the same to me. It isn't the threat to me that pulls at my revenge strings but more because of my parents and the fact that these two hawks were undoubtably the ones who attacked Yves, leaving him battered and bruised, fighting for life in the middle of the forest.

As these images and thoughts stir through my mind, unbeknownst to myself, my talons come closer to my snout, my uncle remaining in my grasp. The smell of his treacherous flesh gets stronger. He kicks and screams as I expose my teeth, ready to sink them into his flesh, the urge overtaking my body, fueled from the fire and anger burning deep within.

"Ava."

I think I hear someone call my name. Disinterested, I push it aside. I'm caught in this moment, longing to destroy these people for what they did to my parents. They stripped me of my parents at such a young age.

What makes it worse—they were my father's blood relatives.

"Ava," someone calls again, barely penetrating my thoughts. "Ava!" It grows louder when I fail to respond.

I blink slowly, trying to push away the thought that someone is saying my name.

"Ava, I know you. You don't want to do this." Something blue flutters in the corner of my eye, and I focus on the kind face of Archangel Gabriel. Worry sets into their eyes even when an understanding smile creeps on their face. The archangel looks deep into my eyes. "Oh, Ava. You don't want to do this. This isn't you." They flap their light-blue wings, a puff of breeze blowing their wavy blond locks from their shoulders. "I can imagine from the form you have taken that what they did was terrible, but you don't want to do this."

The soft, kind words penetrate the thick scales I've built around my heart, tickling at the edges of my searing anger. A slight ripple disturbs the hot hatred simmering within. The sizzling hatred continues to burn in my belly when I gaze at my wide-eyed uncle. Theodore's attention moves from my dragon form to Archangel Gabriel then back to me, not knowing who he should fear the most. Seeing him like this reminds me of what he did to my parents, sparking a new surge of anger to flow through my body. Slowly I lift him closer to my mouth.

"You don't want to do this, Ava." Archangel Gabriel's calming voice worries at the edge of my rage. "I know you don't. Put him down. We'll make sure he pays in a different way. Remember, he's Andre's father. You will cause your cousin pain if you do this."

An image of Andre flashes in my head. I carry a love for my newfound cousin and would hate to cause him the same grief I dealt with when I was a child.

"This is not you. Put him down." The archangel sits on my head then reaches down and touches my eyelid. A deep surge of love and peace jolts through me, and my anger wavers.

Slowly, I lower my uncle, and Archangel Gabriel flies off my head, landing in front of me near my uncle. With slumped shoulders, I change back into my human form.

"That's it, Ava. I need you to come around." The archangel stands next to me, and I collapse to the ground, my knees buckling, and bow my head to the floor. Tears cascade down my face as a mixture of hate and grief flows out in their salty form.

The archangel's gentle hands trace my back, each stroke sending me waves of peace. Rosa runs to Theodore's side, and Henri's father and Jeanne hover together in the corner, a blanket wrapped around their shoulders. Blood trickles down the side of Jeanne's face from her missing ear.

A loud crash sounds from the front door, and Andre charges through the entrance, his mouth agape as he observes the catastrophe. The state of the cottage would be a lot to take in, adding to the presence of Archangel Gabriel leaning over my bent form, their wings fully exposed.

"I heard there was a dragon attack." Andre's eyes land on me then rise to the broken roof. "Yves said it would be you."

It takes all my effort to push myself up from the ground and go to him. "Yves is right. It was me, and if it weren't for Archangel Gabriel, I probably would have killed your parents and everyone in this room."

"Why?" he asks.

"They admitted to killing my parents. I didn't need to read their minds. They proudly admitted they ambushed them and murdered my father before murdering my mother… making her watch."

Andre's eyes land on his father then move to his mother. "You are dead to me. Not only did you use me for information when I was only ten years old and used Yves for information, you murdered your own brother, Ava's father, and her mother."

His parents stare at him in silence.

Andre turns to me. "I'm so sorry."

My body shakes as I touch his arm. "It's not your fault, Andre. You were only a child."

He rests his forehead in his hand, looking ashamed even though I tried to be reassuring.

"Oh, sweetie." Archangel Gabriel wraps an arm over Andre's shoulder. "You were just a child. I can tell you're not like them, and Ava has nothing but pride in you."

Andre stares at the archangel's wings and the androgynous face and frowns, then gazes at me. "Is this the protection angel you were talking about?"

"No. This is Archangel Gabriel. Although they've come to my aid, they're more of a creative angel—a loving and more understanding angel. Not that the other angels aren't. This archangel is more like a friend."

Andre's eyes are wide as he stares at them. "Oh. It's nice to meet you. I guess that's what you say." He looks lost.

Archangel Gabriel chuckles. "It's nice to meet you, too, Andre."

"Are you going to take my parents to hell?" he asks, a thin line creasing his forehead.

"Oh no. That's not my job," Archangel Gabriel says.

Andre gazes at his parents then at the other two. "What are you going to do to them? Surely you must punish them or something. I know they're my parents, but they shouldn't just go free of punishment after doing what they did."

Archangel Gabriel rests their chin between their forefinger and thumb, their eyes deep in thought as they observe the four murderers. "You're right. Something should be done." Archangel Gabriel looks at Andre. "Do you think you would be upset if I made them forget you and anything to do with anybody special in their lives?"

"You mean you're not going to kill them?" Andre asks.

"Oh no." The archangel swipes a dismissive hand. "That would require me to get my hands dirty. Besides, I'm not into killing. I don't like that sort of stuff."

Andre frowns, and a few minutes pass before he answers. "Okay. I think it's a good idea. I don't mind if they forget me. I'm not that close to them anyway."

Archangel Gabriel claps their hands. "Perfect." They nod, indicating the other two. "What about them?"

"I don't think Henri and Yvonne would worry too much about being forgotten either. None of them have been the best of parents—now that I think about it."

The archangel's eyes brighten. "Done. That I can do. I can erase memories. I'll make sure they forget that they hate witches too."

"Really?" Andre asks.

"Yes."

Humming, Archangel Gabriel places a palm on each forehead, not giving the people a chance to dispute it. When finished, the faces of the four adults look blank, almost confused.

The archangel grabs my hand and calls to Andre, "Come. I hear you have a wife who needs a little bit of sweetening." They smirk.

EPILOGUE

Over the next few years, I return to the cottage where my parents once lived. With Yves's help and occasional help from Archangel Gabriel, we demolish the old cottage and build a new one. The thought of moving back to the place that held memories of better times with Zacharias and where Jehan was murdered is too hard. Instead, I decide to tend to my parents' farm. Archangel Gabriel takes several trips, transferring the animals from my farm to my parents' farm. I have few memories of my parents' cottage and want to remain fairly close to Andre. I've grown fond of him, and after Archangel Gabriel wiped all unfounded hatred of witches from Simonne's brain, she has turned into a lovely woman.

After growing accustomed to solitary living, away from the prying eyes of suspicious people, I can't bring myself to live in the village. I'm not completely alone. I build Yves a small place where he can stay whenever he likes. The untalented wizard shape-shifter visits regularly but often feels more at home in the forest treetops, stopping in regularly for meals and repaying my generosity by helping with the farm.

The years pass by, taking with them the ones I have grown to love. Each loss hurts, yet as Zacharias said, I am better off for knowing them during their short lives. It is the curse of witches and angels with their extended lives. With each loved one who passes, another rises, just like how I grow to love Andre's son. I revel in watching him grow and making sure he's safe.

After a few hundred years, Yves passes, and I bury him next to my parents. I miss the old shape-shifting wizard and his strange ways.

Over the passing years, the angels regularly call for help to defeat demons. One thing that doesn't change is my ache over the separation from Zacharias. I hope each time I assist the angels that he will miraculously join us or that he'll ask for me one time when he rises to the surface of the Tatev Monastery, but it never happens. My heart yearns for him and aches over the pain he holds, even after a thousand years—my immortal loved one trapped in a world of depression. The tear in my heart won't mend knowing he isn't getting better.

My progress is slow, but even as a witch, I age over the thousand years that pass. My reactions slow, and the struggle to help the angels proves harder as my body stiffens. I get old, though age doesn't dull my senses. A strange sensation grows in my awareness. At first it's faint, but over a period of years, it grows until one day it dawns on me as I change into my dragon form. Another witch with a heart as pure as my mother's is going to bear a child to a shape-shifter.

This child won't just have the blood of a shape-shifter and witch. My dragon senses another rare shape-shifting dragon is about to be born. I don't want the child to go through everything I did. I want them to have the best start possible, especially against the witches of the coven. Although shape-shifting biases vary against others who aren't shape-shifters, the witch covens remain defiant. It saddens my heart to think that very few witches will open their minds to accepting others.

After changing back into my human form, I unpack my special spell books I crafted while growing into the woman I've become. I hold the golden leafed bobby pin to my chest then kiss it, my thoughts trailing to Zacharias, before placing it on top of the books. Pulling out a large piece of shape-shifting material, I wrap the books within the fabric and tie them together securely with a ribbon. Pushing my hands on my lower back, I stand, a dull ache traveling up my spine with each straightened vertebra.

A hand grasps my bent elbow, and I startle.

"Archangel Michael!" I hold a hand over my heart.

Slight amusement mixed with compassion flicks through his sapphire-blue eyes. "Sorry, Ava. I didn't mean to scare you. You were so engrossed in what you were doing that I guess you didn't hear me."

"I'm not as young as I used to be. My hearing is probably going too. Although, what also surprises me is that I was thinking I needed to contact you somehow." I lift an eyebrow at him. "Can you read my thoughts?"

He chuckles. "You know I can if I want to, but I wasn't reading them today. Why?"

"Then how did you know I needed to see you?"

He shrugs. "Honestly, I was coming to see you."

"Oh?"

"As you know, our numbers are diminishing to a dangerous level, and you're getting on in years, and it's becoming harder for you to fight with us."

My gaze falls to the ground. "I'm sorry."

He clasps my arm gently. "No. No. That isn't your fault. We knew this would happen eventually. Whatever you gave us is a bonus. However, my consciousness has led me to you today. It's niggling at me, telling me that you have the answer to help with our future."

My knees give, and he catches me before I crumple to the floor. He leads me to the nearest couch.

"That's a lot to lay on an old lady."

The archangel helps me sit. "I know. You don't have to think of something straight away. I thought I would set your thought cogs turning and maybe you would come up with something while I'm here. If not, you can tell me during another visit."

A puff of breeze drifts through the open window, cooling the beads of sweat on my forehead. I wipe them away with my sleeve. The burden is vast yet one I won't refuse. The parcel on the table catches my eye as I think of ways to help. My thoughts are broken by Michael's voice.

"You said you needed to see me?"

I nod. "Yes." Indicating the package on the table, I say, "I need you to deliver that parcel."

He frowns. "Who to?"

"There's a witch. She's only young, but I can sense her and the offspring she will bear. I want her to have those to give them a better start in life. She's not surrounded by loved ones, as I was."

"What is it?"

"My two spell books and some of the shape-shifting material I designed."

Michael gazes curiously at me. "Another shape-shifting witch?"

"Not this witch but her child."

Archangel Michael's face lights up in a smile. "Is she going to be as strong as you?"

I cross my legs. "Possibly. If my dragon senses are correct."

His smile brightens, and I hold up a finger.

"But I have a sense it's going to be delayed."

The archangel's golden leather Roman uniform squeaks as he collects the package off the table. Silence falls between us as he sits with his hands resting on the parcel, and his expression turns distant.

A strange thought crosses my mind, and I let the idea run. "Do our souls live on after we die?"

A stunned look crosses over the archangel's face,

then his shoulders soften. "Oh, Ava. If you're worried about your soul after you die, then don't. You—"

Holding up a hand, I stop him and smile. "It's not for me."

He frowns before his eyebrows rise. "Ahh. For your parents and Jehan then. Yes. Their souls were reborn."

A strange peace takes over my heart. "As humans?"

"Yes."

"That would have been nice to know when I was grieving."

"Sorry. I thought one of us would have told you."

I shake my head in understanding. "It actually wasn't why I was asking." Another puzzled expression fills Archangel Michael's face. "How many times does the soul come back?"

"Many times. Sometimes as a human, sometimes as an animal."

I swing my crossed leg a few times, deep in thought. "I understand that being an angel is a very honorable thing."

A deep frown creases the archangel's forehead. "Yes."

"And you can tell when a human soul is pure or evil."

"Yes." The creases deepen.

I uncross my legs and recross them the opposite direction, then fiddle with the material on my skirt, feeling the archangel's curious gaze on me. "Why don't you turn humans into angels?"

"What?" The word shoots out of the protector angel's mouth, laced with shock.

I hold up a gnarled finger, indicating for him to wait. "Not just any human, but one that has a pure heart and has been murdered three times—each time remaining pure of heart. The human population has increased rapidly. Surely, there should be some that remain that way, even in this modern age and all the temptation and evils that come with it."

The deep thought creases return to the archangel's face. Slowly he nods. "There are some." He stands, placing the parcel on his seat, and paces. "It may work. I'll have to present the idea to the other archangels, though. Thank you." He leans over and hugs me as I sit. "Take care of yourself. You are getting frail. I can feel your bones."

I smile wanly. "It's all part of getting old."

Archangel Michael grabs the parcel. "I'll deliver this to Rita." His body breaks down into particles and vanishes.

I shake my head. I didn't tell him her name. He probably already knows something is special about her and worked it out after I filled in what I'd picked up.

Another decade passes, and one late autumn, as I tend to my animals, throwing food over the fence and watching the chickens race to the vegetable scraps, a male voice sounds behind me.

"I see chickens are still your favorite."

I freeze. The rich male voice is tender, holding sparks of familiarity from my childhood. It digs up the long-term wish that I'd banished, for the emotions were too strong. Clenching my teeth, I gaze in the direction of the voice. My eyes are no longer what they used to be, and the image is clouded with haze. I blink, focusing on a golden breastplate covering a robust chest and shoulders. Blond hair falls to the shoulders shadowed by majestic white wings that expand broadly behind him. I blink, trying to push away the dream before me. It doesn't shift, and my jaw drops.

"Zacharias? Is that you?"

His face distorts with pain. He inches closer, and I flinch. "Yes, Ava. It's me. I'm so sorry. I heard I've been a grump and shut you out."

I stare at his powerful and beautiful wings and the face that hasn't aged a day.

"But I heard you were broken. I heard you had turned old from anger and hostility."

"That's true. It's why I did not see you. It was the anger and hostility that pushed you away. I've missed you."

As I gaze at the ground, tears trickle down my cheeks, getting stuck in the creases lining my aged face. I raise a gnarled hand to wipe them away, catching sight of the old limb before me. Last time I saw Zacharias, my skin was smooth and young, not much older than twenty-one years. Now my skin is withered, and I'm no longer young. So many years have passed. So much time to hang on to this hurt and sorrow. "How could you possibly know who I am? What makes you think I'm Ava? I don't look the slightest bit like the young girl you knew."

He clasps the hand I observe. "Years may have changed your looks, but I know it's you. I can sense your heart." He lifts my chin with his hand. "And I have missed your heart."

He opens his arms, and tears stream down my face as I press against his chest. He wraps his arms around me, cocooning me in his beautiful white wings, securing me against his heart.

"I've missed you so much." My fingers fiddle with the edges of his golden breastplate.

"I've missed you too."

I push back from him and restudy his form. He is young, exactly how I remember him. "What happened? They said you were broken and anger turned you old."

"Recently, Michael gave me some new trainees. I refused at first. They were from human blood. I had grown to despise humans, blaming them for my condition."

Confusion clouds my face as I look at him.

He explains. "I thought you didn't come to visit me, even though Michael told me you had. I thought you had left me, and I saw my condition as a side effect from a mission to protect humans."

He must have read the confusion on my face.

"It's a twisted way of thinking, I know. But I despised you because I thought you had rejected me. I was so wrong. I'm sorry. It was the earthbound curse speaking to me." His face looks as though it could break. "I was so angry." He pauses, watching me closely. "As you know, we have lost many angels to the battle with demons. We were desperate for more angels. The archangels created a new recruiting process. Any innocent humans that were murdered in three different lives were recruited into our fledgling program."

A smile creeps on my face, and I know my idea was put to use.

Zacharias continues. "Michael needed help training some of his because his duties were not giving him enough time to train them properly. He brought three of these humans-turned-angels to me at the monastery. I refused at first because they were humans, but despite myself, they won their way into my heart, just like you. Not only that, they went to the ends of the earth and to the corners of hell to find my wings, doing everything within their power to break my curse of being earth-bound. Once again, humans changed my life."

"You're getting soppy, old man," a female calls from behind him.

I pull back, glancing underneath his beautiful wings to get a good look. A thin blond female in yellow body-suit clothing I'm unaccustomed to seeing stands behind him with pale-yellow wings. A clip fastens her golden-blond hair away from her face, showing off her golden-brown eyes. Her face is beautiful, almost perfect. She stands with her feet shoulder width apart as though ready to spring into action at any time. "Ava, this is my partner."

I search his face. "Partner?" I had heard in the

modern age that humans no longer needed to marry. They had a new word for unwedded people, partner. But Zacharias told me that angels weren't allowed to marry. I hadn't even thought about the females when I suggested they turn humans into angels.

Zacharias studies my face and throws his head back and laughs. Oh, how I've missed that laugh.

"Yes. My partner. She is one of those human angels and the love of my life."

FREE DOWNLOAD

Find out more
about the
Gatekeeper...

Get updates & notifications of giveaways

CLICK HERE TO GET STARTED: FREE COPY OF THE Gatekeeper

Or visit http://www.katrinacopebooks.com

Sign up for my newsletter and receive updates about my fantasy books and notification of giveaways.

ACKNOWLEDGMENTS

I would like to thank my readers for their patience and understanding. This book has been a long time in the making. Life threw in a few curveballs, accelerating health issues and messing with my concentration. But these things are not going to hold me back from my love of writing and creating new worlds.

I appreciate the help I received from my alpha readers and the input from my editor, Amanda K., and my proofreader, Laura K. I'm forever grateful for the editing, writing tips, and suggestions they give me.

Thank you to all of my readers who love my work, and continue to read my stories. There are many more books to come.

YOUR SAY

Enjoy this book? You can make a big difference.

Honest reviews of my books help bring them to the attention of other readers.

If you've enjoyed this book, I'd be grateful if you could spend a few minutes leaving a review (it can be as short as you like).

The review can be left on Amazon & Goodreads.

Thank you very much.

ABOUT THE AUTHOR

Katrina is an author of several Young Adult and Preteen/Middle Grade novels. Many of her books achieving Amazon's Best Sellers Rank – a few even as high as number one.

She resides in Queensland, Australia. Her three teenaged boys and husband of over twenty years treat her like a princess. Unfortunately though, this princess still has to do domestic chores.

From birth, she has been a very creative person and has spent many years travelling the world and observing many different personalities and cultures. Her favourite personalities have been the strange ones, yet the ones under the radar also hold a place in her heart.

During her last extensive travels, she spent 16 nights in a bomb shelter on a Kibbutz 8 kilometers off the Lebanese border. It was to avoid Katyusha bombs that the resident volunteers decided to name her after (she is still trying to work out why).

Katrina's online home is at www.katrinacopebooks.com

You can connect with Katrina on:

- facebook.com/Author.Katrina.Cope
- twitter.com/Katrina_R_Cope
- instagram.com/katrina_cope_author
- bookbub.com/profile/katrina-cope
- pinterest.com/katrinacope56

BOOKS BY KATRINA COPE

Pre-Teen Books

The Sanctum Series

JAYDEN'S CYBERMOUNTAIN

SCARLET'S ESCAPE

TAYLOR'S PLIGHT

ERIC & THE BLACK AXES

ADRIANNA'S SURGE

~~~~~

Young Adult Urban Fantasy

Afterlife Series

FLEDGLING

THE TAKING

ANGELIC RETRIBUTION

DIVIDED PATHS

TRUTH HUNTER

Afterlife Novelette

THE GATEKEEPER

~~~~~

Young Adult Urban Paranormal Fantasy

Supernatural Evolvement Series

(Associated with the Afterlife Series)

WITCH'S LEGACY (Prequel)

AALIYAH

~~~~~

Young Adult Norse Mythology Fantasy

Valkyrie Academy Dragon Alliance

MARKED

CHOSEN

VANISHED

SCORNED

INFLICTED

EMPOWERED

AMBUSHED

WARNED

ABDUCTED

BESIEGED

DECEIVED